CURSES & VOWS

LASHELL COLLINS

1

"Are you ready for this, baby?"

Detective Isaac Taylor stuffed the last of his barbecue pork taco into his mouth and stared at the most beautiful woman in the world.

Was he ready?

Was she kidding?

He swallowed his mouthful and licked the sauce from his lips.

"I am more than ready to marry you, darlin'. But you already know that."

They had just come from the courthouse, where they'd met in the middle of the day to obtain their marriage license. Now, they sat at a picnic table in the food truck lot where he'd treated her to a quick lunch before they both went back to work.

As Mondays went, this was a pretty freaking good one.

Sidney wiped her hands with a napkin.

"I am more than ready to marry you too. But I'm not talking about the wedding. I mean the craziness. It's about to begin."

"The craziness?"

"Yep."

"Hmm. What is this craziness of which you speak?"

Sidney grinned at him, and his day got even brighter. How in the world a social misfit like him had scored a gorgeous, smart, sexy woman like her, he would never know. But he'd be forever grateful.

"You know what I'm talking about. Weddings always make people crazy."

"I've heard the rumors."

He downed the last of his soda and smiled at her.

"And we both have family coming in this week. It's about to get really hectic. I'm glad I decided to take the week off from work. I have a million things to do before the wedding."

Sidney sighed, and Isaac just knew that she was running her to-do list through her head.

"I'm really grateful that Zoe let me take the week off."

"Well, just make sure to keep in mind what we've already agreed to, okay? You and I are not going to get caught up in all the craziness, remember? That's why we sent your family a list of five-star area hotels to choose from, and we set my grandad up at Adam's place, where he and Bree have way more room, and a maid. That way we don't have to worry about hosting anyone at our house this week."

"Yes, I know. And everyone agreed and understood. But I've got the family brunch at the hotel tomorrow when everyone gets in. Oh! Which reminds me that I need to call there and finalize the brunch menu. And we've got the bachelor and bachelorette parties coming up, and the rehearsal dinner. And we have to..."

"Sidney."

Isaac's tone was firm when he cut her off. He reached out and took both of her hands in his own, and looked into her eyes.

"It's all going to be great. Don't let the process stress you out, okay? We're in the home stretch now. The location's set, the florist and caterer are booked, the DJ's ready to rock. Your gown is being altered. Everything is done. Let's just relax and enjoy it, all right?"

She sighed, and Isaac could tell she tried to stop the smile that was slowly spreading over her luscious lips.

"All right. But you do realize that telling a bride not to stress out five days before her wedding is like telling a bird not to fly, don't you?"

Ike grinned. "Well, maybe I'll just have to come up with a few ideas to keep you relaxed and happy, huh?"

"Intriguing thought. What have you got in mind?"

"Oh, I don't know." Still holding her hands in his, he ran his thumbs back and forth over her knuckles. "Maybe a little preview of what to expect on our honeymoon."

He leaned in and kissed her lips. He couldn't stop himself.

"I like the sound of that. Especially since you won't tell me where we're going."

"Nope. You get no hints."

"But you know that I've never been anywhere but here and California. The states I drove through to get from there to here were just a blur, since I wasn't exactly sightseeing at the time. At least tell me if we're going to another state?"

"No hints."

"Come on, Ike! I don't even know what to pack."

"You don't need to pack anything but a bathing suit, darlin'. A bathing suit and a toothbrush. That's it. And you probably won't even be wearing the bathing suit much."

"So... we're going someplace with a beach?"

She gasped and her face lit up with a guess.

"Are you taking me back to California because I miss the Pacific Ocean?"

Isaac chuckled and opened his mouth to reiterate that he wasn't about to give her any clues, when his cellphone rang. He held up a finger — the universal symbol for wait a second — and pulled the phone from his pocket. It was police dispatch.

"Taylor."

"Good afternoon, Detective Sergeant. You and Detective Vega

are needed at the bowling alley downtown. There's been a shooting. Officers on scene say there are two bodies and possible wounded. EMTs and CSU have already been dispatched."

"Okay."

The word came out on a sigh.

"Detective Vega is not with me at the moment, so you'll need to call him. I'll be there as soon as I can."

He ended the call and looked at Sidney.

"I've got to go. Dead bodies. Two of them, at the bowling alley."

"Homicide in the broad daylight?"

"It happens."

They stood and gathered up their trash.

"Well, I need to get going too. I promised to swing by the shelter for a bit to drop off some worksheets for the kids and clear some things off my desk before the wedding."

"What happened to taking the week off?"

"I am off. This is just going to take a few minutes. An hour, tops. The shelter is pretty full right now, and I feel kind of like I'm leaving them in the lurch."

"Oh yeah?"

"Six adults and seven children. There's a lot of abuse going on out there unfortunately. A couple of the residents are getting ready for court dates. A few others who are going through coaching for job interviews. And I'm tutoring some of the children in math and reading. It's been crazy."

They tossed their trash into the bin, and Isaac wrapped his arm around her waist, pulled her close, and walked her to her car.

"So what's going to happen next week when you're busy making love on a beach somewhere?"

She smiled at him and his stomach did this weird, decidedly un-manly, quivering thing.

"Is that what I'll be doing next week, Detective?"

Her voice was flirtatious, and Isaac grinned and opened her driver's door.

"Oh, trust me. There's going to be a whole lot of that going on, Ms. Fairchild. And I'm dearly sorry that we can only take two weeks away."

He leaned in and nibbled on her neck, and Sidney giggled.

"Well, I imagine we'll make the most of those two weeks. And to answer your question, Zoe's offered Julie some overtime pay to take some extra hours the next two weeks while I'm gone. And we've had Beth, one of the residents, doing some filing and light office work for the past few weeks too."

"Good." Isaac kissed her lips. "Because I don't want you preoccupied with work concerns once I've got you all to myself."

One last kiss, this one lingering. Then he sighed, and she slid into the car.

"Gotta go. You be careful going to Hope House."

"I will. See you tonight, husband-to-be."

"Love you, wife-to-be."

"I love you back. Be safe."

Isaac watched her drive away before he got into his own car and headed off to another crime scene.

2

*I*saac pulled up at the bowling alley where a large portion of the parking lot had been sectioned off with bright yellow police tape. The place was teeming with people in uniforms — police officers were keeping the growing crowd of gawkers at bay, while paramedics were tending to a person who appeared wounded. On the ground, lay two bodies, and the crime scene techs were hovering over them. Off to the left he saw the news trucks moving in.

"Detective Sergeant."

An eager-looking officer guarding the scene snapped to attention. He was either a rookie or a detective hopeful, Isaac thought. Maybe both. Either way, Isaac acknowledged him with a nod and slipped under the police tape. He spotted his partner across the parking lot already looking over the scene, and he headed that way.

"What have we got, Pete?"

"Witnesses say there was no altercation. Guy just follows a small group of people out of the bowling alley and opens fire. Then he takes off."

"Can witnesses describe the shooter? Or the car he took off in?"

Pete shrugged a shoulder.

"I just got here and got the scoop from a uniform. I haven't questioned anyone yet."

He turned and looked Isaac in the face.

"You and Sidney get the license?"

Isaac grinned at the mention of it. He couldn't help himself. He was marrying the woman of his dreams in just a few days.

"Yeah. We're all set."

He turned his attention to the bodies on the ground and moved in closer, digging a pair of blue latex gloves from his pockets and pulling them on.

The gloves brought an unpleasant memory of the thick nitrile gloves he used to wear at crime scenes like this. All in an effort to keep from touching the dead bodies and having a flash of the victim's last few moments of life.

But all that had changed now.

Everything in his life had changed the day Sidney floated in and brought her sunshine and warmth.

He stepped carefully beside a CSU tech who was taking pictures of the body. She looked up at him.

"We found a couple of shell casings, Detective. Look like .45s to me."

She pointed a few feet away to where she'd marked the shells, and Isaac walked over and gingerly knelt to examine it. He studied the casing without touching it.

"Definitely a .45," he mumbled, and stood. He turned back to the tech. "Was this a robbery?"

"We haven't gotten that far yet, sir. You're welcome to check."

Isaac glanced at Pete and nodded toward the body.

Pete understood his non-verbal perfectly and quickly stepped over to the body. Lightly, he patted the corpse's pockets with gloved hands and pulled out a wallet. Isaac watched him flip through it.

"Victim's name is Derrick Powell and he..." Pete checked the wallet thoroughly, "was not robbed."

He handed the wallet over to Isaac and then went over to the other body.

Isaac flipped through the wallet himself noting all cash and credit cards still there. The tech handed him two evidence bags.

"Thanks."

Pete came back holding the second victim's wallet.

"Ian Pembroke. Also not robbed."

"So if it wasn't robbery, maybe it was personal." Isaac handed Pete one of the evidence bags. "Where are our witnesses?"

"All inside with Officer Drake," Pete said, placing the wallet inside the bag.

"All right. Let's leave CSU to it and get started."

Inside the bowling alley a group of six people sat silently while Officer Drake looked on. Isaac gestured to him.

"Stay here while we separate them out one by one for questioning."

"Sure thing, Detective."

Over the next hour they spoke to the girl who worked the shoe rental counter, the man who ran the concession stand, the owner of the bowling alley, and three patrons who'd been bowling with the two dead victims earlier in the day. By the time they had questioned them all, Isaac felt no closer to understanding what had happened than he had before they'd begun. He looked at Pete and shook his head.

"So these two over here were bowling with Pembroke." He gestured to two of the bowlers.

"Yes, and that one was bowling with Powell."

"And according to them, Powell and Pembroke did not know each other."

"So they say."

"We'll need to pick them both apart and see if that holds up."

"Yep."

"Did you notice that all of our witnesses describe the gun in great detail?"

"Oh, yeah. Hard to ignore a description like that. Gold plated and ornate. Fancy grips. But they can't say what the shooter looked like. What the hell is that about?"

Isaac shook his head. "I don't know, but it doesn't sound... normal."

"I'll say. I mean, none of them can even say for certain that the shooter was even inside the bowling alley. Some of them say he was and that he followed them out. Others say the shooter was outside and opened fire as they exited the building."

Isaac gestured to the pool of witnesses again.

"Yes, but the girl from the shoe rental counter didn't recall seeing him at all. She said that she rented bowling shoes to five people. So if the shooter was inside at any time, he didn't bowl."

Isaac turned to Officer Drake and motioned to the witnesses with a nod of his head.

"They're all free to go, but make sure we have contact information on all of them."

"Yes, sir."

He and Pete left the building, and Isaac ran a hand over the back of his neck.

"Two groups of people who claim not to know each other, both leaving the bowling alley at the same time."

"And a shooter who may or may not have been inside watching them bowl," Pete offered.

Isaac glanced over to where the CSU techs had completed pictures and were now actively gathering evidence.

"And none of those people can describe the shooter, yet they all perfectly describe the gun used." He looked at Pete. "Something about that just doesn't sound right."

"Nope. But the gun sounds beautiful." Pete grinned.

Isaac smirked at him. "I'll see you back at the house."

———

"Okay, I've left the worksheets here in this folder marked school, and they're separated by grade already, but to make it easier on everyone I've also written the children's names on them. So all you have to do is grab and go. There's enough worksheets there for the entire two weeks I'll be gone, so the children will each have something to work on. I also left some fun coloring and activity sheets in their packets."

"Sidney, you're too much," Zoe exclaimed. "Teaching the resident's children isn't even part of your job description. And most of them are still able to go to school every day."

"Well, I know, but then there are ones like Beth's daughter, Kylee. She still can't send that girl back to school what with Hank threatening to grab her and run. Oh! That reminds me. I also brought a few books for Kylee."

She dug into her tote bag and pulled out three paperback books from a popular children's series and set them beside the school folder with a sticky note bearing Kylee's name.

"Make sure to let Beth know that these are here. They should help keep Kylee busy while I'm gone."

Zoe sighed. "You're spoiling that girl."

"Who, Kylee? Or Beth?"

"Both."

"I just feel bad for them. I mean, can you imagine, Zoe? Being afraid to send your child to school for fear of your highly abusive husband snatching that child and leaving the state with them? Or the country?"

"I wish the cops could find that jackass. How is it that they can't seem to locate him, yet he still manages to get threatening notes and messages to Beth and terrorize her?"

"I don't know. But it's all so sad."

"It is indeed." Zoe stretched and then popped up. "Oh, this came for you in the mail. It's a postcard from someone named Angela Mason."

Sidney's stomach did an anxious bounce, and she spun around and looked at Zoe.

"Angela Mason? Really?"

She hurried over and took the postcard, reading it eagerly.

"Oh, my gosh!"

"What is it?"

Sidney glanced around to make sure no one was in earshot, then she looked at Zoe.

"It's from Ann."

Zoe gasped. "I had no idea. What's it say?"

Sidney rushed to the door and closed it. Then she walked back to Zoe's desk and said softly, "She and her kids have settled in a small town just outside Calgary."

"Canada?"

Zoe sounded mildly shocked, and Sidney nodded and kept reading.

"She's found a job and a small apartment. She's even managed to obtain a work visa. They're doing well."

"Oh, that's so great!"

The relief gushed down over her like a waterfall, and Sidney smiled and walked over to the shredder, sticking the postcard through.

"Wait! What are you doing? Why did you destroy it?"

"It's part of the plan. It has to be done."

Sidney watched understanding dawn on her boss's face.

"Of course. I get it. Very clever."

Sidney nodded and sat down at her desk. Now, also according to the plan, she would have to get a message to Ann's elderly mother, just as they had agreed.

"I still can't believe you did this, Sidney. That you actually pulled it off."

"What do you mean?"

"Well, it just all seems so risky. Gutsy. I'm not sure I would've had the courage to send someone off like that. Not knowing what was in store for them."

"You make it sound like I pushed her." Sidney shook her head. "I didn't push her into this, Zoe. She came to me for help."

"Oh, no, no. That's not what I meant. It's just that... well, we all know from experience that running is risky."

"True. But I think staying in a highly abusive situation is riskier by far. Especially when you put two small children into the mix."

"I still can't believe he threatened to kill her babies."

"I know." Sidney leaned back in her chair and thought about how Ann's voice had trembled when she'd told her that her husband, Donald, had threatened to kill their children after she'd asked him not to hit her in front of them.

"Well, thankfully, he's behind bars now, and there's no way he'll ever get a hint of where they are."

"I wish my sister, Hope, had run." Zoe's voice sounded far away, and she stared off into the distance. "Anywhere in the world. I just wish she was still alive and safe."

Sidney watched her and placed a hand over her own heart. She knew that Zoe often thought of the sister who'd been killed by her abusive husband.

"You know, Sidney... we should think about making your services a staple here at Hope House. One we won't actively advertise or offer. But it'll be there, silently on the menu."

"But if we don't actively offer it, how will they know it's an option?"

Zoe looked her in the eyes. "Oh, they'll know. There's already whispers and speculation around here about where Ann disappeared to. Word of mouth will do the advertising for us."

"You do know that I didn't charge Ann any money for my help, right?"

"Of course. We don't need the money. Just the satisfaction that comes from helping an abused woman feel empowered again."

Sidney smiled at her boss. Sometimes, Zoe had the ability to really surprise her.

"I love that idea."

A soft, but urgent knock sounded on the door and they both looked up when Beth rushed in.

"Oh, Beth, good!" Sidney smiled at her. "I've left some things..."

"You've got to help me!"

The woman was near frantic and Sidney stared at her.

"Hank won't stop. He keeps sending me messages saying he's going to grab Kylee and run, and I'll never see her again. He's getting worse and the cops still can't find him. They keep saying they can't track the phone he's texting from. Can you help me get away, Sidney? Please! Can you help me, you know... the way you did for Ann?"

Speechless, Sidney looked at Zoe and felt her heart drop down into her stomach.

3

"*B*eth, slow down."

Sidney led the distraught young woman to a chair and motioned for her to sit.

"Take a deep breath and try to calm down, okay?"

"I can't calm down," Beth said, taking a deep breath anyway. "He's coming for my baby! He wants to take her and run."

"Beth..."

"No. You don't understand. He molested her!"

All the air left Sidney's lungs.

She stared at Beth with a hollow pit in her stomach.

"It's the reason we fought that night."

Tears rolled down Beth's face. Tears she didn't even attempt to stop.

"For months Kylee hadn't been herself. Her grades started to slip. She wasn't the same happy girl she'd always been. I thought maybe she was being bullied in school. I even went to talk to her teacher about it."

She paused and wiped her face with the back of her hand.

Zoe rushed over with a box of tissues and Beth took a handful.

"Kylee finally told me what had been happening. What Hank was doing to her. And I hate myself because I didn't know."

She wiped more tears.

"How the hell did I not know!" she screamed, her voice echoing around the office in an angry wail.

"How did I not know he was hurting my baby?"

Beth broke down, sobs wracking her thin frame.

"Oh, honey."

Zoe pulled over a chair and sat next to her, wrapping her arms around her.

Sidney wiped her own tears and then pulled over her desk chair and sat in front of Beth. She took the woman's hand.

"Beth, I'm so sorry. I had no idea."

"When she told me, I knew. I never questioned it. I believed her. I knew she was telling me the truth. And I hated myself for bringing that man into her life."

"Hank is not Kylee's father?"

Beth shook her head.

"Kylee's dad died when she was just three. I met Hank a few months later. From the beginning he called her his special girl. I thought he was so good with her. He helped me raise her. He's the only dad she's ever known. How could he do this?"

She broke down into sobs again, and Sidney lightly squeezed her hand.

"What did you do after Kylee told you what Hank had done?"

"I confronted him. At first he tried to deny it. Then he went crazy. Started hitting me. He always hits me, but that night it was vicious. He said that we couldn't leave him, that he would have us both and there was nothing I could do to stop him. Kylee was hiding when he was beating me. I know it's the only reason he didn't take her when he ran from the cops."

The room was silent for a long time, save for the soft sound of weeping.

Sidney and Zoe exchanged a look while Beth cried.

Finally Sidney took a breath.

"Beth. If I agree to help you, there are some things you're going to need. And some things you're going to need to hear."

Beth perked up, still wiping tears.

"You'll help me?"

"I will help you. But my time right now is limited. I'm getting married and leaving for two weeks."

"Oh, I can't wait that long, Sidney, I just can't. Three more weeks of Hank terrorizing Kylee and me? And what if he does something crazy like break in here or find us when we're out somewhere? Please! Can't you do something before you go?"

Sidney sighed.

"Possibly. That's really going to depend on you."

"On me?"

"Yes. On how much money you can scrape together in just a few days. That's number one on my list of things you're going to need. False papers cost money. So do plane tickets, or bus fare, and gas for cars. And that's just one of the things you need to think about."

"I have some money. It's the money from Billy's life insurance. He was my husband. Kylee's real dad. I never let Hank know that I had it because I knew he'd just drink it away. It's in the bank in Kylee's name. Is $250 thousand enough?"

Sidney stared at her and then smiled.

"Yes, that should be more than enough."

"Then you'll help me? I'll pay whatever you charged Ann."

"You'll pay exactly what I charged Ann. Zero dollars. And yes, I'll help you. But there are some things we have to talk about first."

"What things? I'll do anything."

"First, you have to understand that if you go through with this, you'll be leaving everyone you know behind. Family, friends, any support system you may have in place here is all gone."

"That's okay. I don't have anyone. If I did, Kylee and I wouldn't be here."

"Second, you and Kylee need to choose new names. Steer clear of any name that has a family significance for you. No grandmother's maiden name or anything like that. Doing that only makes it easier for Hank to find you. We don't want that."

"Right."

Beth nodded, but she was beginning to look overwhelmed.

"Third, you're going to need to pick two cities. One to run to, and one to say you're from whenever people ask you. And they will ask."

"Two cities? Got it."

"You're going to want to learn all you can about your fake hometown, so that you're not scrambling when someone asks you the simplest of questions."

"That makes sense."

"I'm going to need to take some pictures of you and Kylee, for the false papers."

"False papers. You said that before. What does that mean?"

"You're going to need things like a driver's license from your fake hometown with your new name on it. A birth certificate for both you and Kylee. Passports if you choose a city in a different country. Things like that."

"Oh, my gosh. So many details I never would've thought about on my own."

"Neither would I."

Zoe sounded impressed, and she looked at Sidney with a new appreciation in her eyes.

"Sidney, you've put a lot of thought into this."

"Yes, I have. These are tactics I used when I ran from my abusive husband. They kept me safe and under the radar for nearly two years. The name thing... that's what tripped me up. It's how Damien found me. Don't make that mistake."

Beth nodded and stared at her intensely.

"When do we start?"

"We just did. I'll take those pics of you and Kylee now, and I'll contact my guy about the papers. He's good and he works fast. So, be ready."

Sidney stood, and to her surprise Beth leaped up and locked her in a bear hug.

"Thank you so much, Sidney! Thank you for helping me keep my little girl safe."

"You're welcome."

"I'll go splash some water on my face and get Kylee in here for those pictures."

"Okay."

When she was gone, Sidney looked at Zoe.

"Did I just agree to facilitate her running from her abuser the week of my wedding?"

"Yes, you did."

"Why did I do that? I have a million other things to do this week!"

"Because helping women escape their abusers is your new calling. And this abuser happens to be molesting a little girl that you've grown very fond of. You couldn't say no."

Sidney sighed. "I wonder if she told the police about Kylee's claims."

"Claims? You don't believe her?"

"Oh, of course, I believe her. But I imagine they'd have to examine Kylee to determine Hank's guilt. Or, at least to determine that molestation had taken place."

"And I doubt Beth would want to put Kylee through that."

"What mother would?"

"Right? Poor thing."

"Well, I need to take these pics and contact my guy, and then get out of here. I have so much to do. I can't believe I just added to my list. But you're right. I couldn't say no."

"Sidney, I'm here. I mean, I'll help in any way I can. What's next after you contact this guy?"

"I send him the pictures, along with all the information."

"Meaning?"

"Meaning new names, new birthplaces, dates. Exactly what papers she'll need. Then he contacts me when they're ready. We meet in a public place for the exchange. Then Beth decides where she's headed to, and I help her get to the bus station, or the airport, or whatever."

"I could do the exchange for you."

"No." Sidney shook her head. "I just established a rapport with this guy. I wouldn't want to spring a new face on him so soon."

"That makes sense. I can put Beth and Kylee on the bus or plane or whatever, when the time comes."

Sidney smiled at her. "I will keep that in mind."

4

*B*ack at the station, Isaac and Pete got to work on the two shooting victims, looking into their backgrounds and known associates, trying to find any connection between the two men.

After a solid two hours of work, Isaac looked up and sighed.

"Tell me you've got something, Pete."

Pete sat back in his chair and shook his head.

"Nothing. There is nothing that connects Derrick Powell to Ian Pembroke. No red flags in his finances. Nothing that would make him a target for anybody."

Isaac tossed the pencil he was fiddling with onto his desk.

"I'm coming up empty on Pembroke too. Nothing unusual with his finances or on his social media. And no connections to Derrick Powell. Seems our witnesses' assertions that the two vics didn't know each other is correct."

"Which would make this a random shooting. But why?"

Isaac shook his head.

"That's what we have to figure out. And with no leads on the shooter, we've got nothing."

"That is not what I wanted to hear, Sergeant."

Isaac and Pete looked up to see Gavin Hayes heading for their desks.

"Two dead bodies, shot down in broad daylight, and zero suspects?"

Gavin did not sound pleased.

"I know how it sounds, Lieu, but..."

"No car descriptions? Camera footage? Anything?"

"Not so far. We do have the IT department checking security footage from the bowling alley parking lot and a couple of the surrounding businesses, but not one of our witnesses can give us a description of the shooter."

Gavin let out a sigh heavy with disgust, and Isaac could feel his boss' frustration.

"Well, a call just came in. There's been another shooting downtown at Birdie's Tavern. I'm giving it to you because it sounds too similar to what you've already got."

"And here I thought it was going to be a lazy Monday with only one open case on my desk before my honeymoon."

"And speaking of that other case...?"

There was a question on the end of that dangling sentence, and Isaac knew what Hayes was getting at. The open case in question was a man from a wealthy family — Gregory Townsend — found dead four days ago in the study of the house that he shared with his young widow, Susan. She hadn't been home at the time, and there was no evidence of forced entry, no evidence of a struggle. The man had simply sat down in front of the large flatscreen and died.

Isaac sighed as he stood.

"I know what you're asking, Lieu, and we don't have any updates for you yet on that one either. We've questioned all the players there."

"A few of them multiple times," Pete interjected with the droll sarcasm Isaac was coming to appreciate.

"Every one of them made mention of this family curse that

the victim spoke about often. Some say he would lament the curse, while others say he spoke of it like it was inevitable. A fact of his life that he knew he couldn't escape. And Hiroshi says the autopsy shows the man was healthy. I'm starting to wonder if this death is even homicide."

"And yet the wife insists that it is," Gavin sighed.

Isaac responded with a shoulder shrug.

"Assuming it is," Gavin continued, "what's your theory?"

Isaac cocked his head and glanced around.

"Everyone in his life knew about this so-called curse placed on his great-grandfather by a supposed witch. A curse that makes all the men in his family drop dead at a young age. He apparently talked about it all the time. Assuming that it was in fact homicide, I'd say someone is using this alleged curse as the perfect cover-up for a murder. We just don't know how to prove that yet. I've asked Hiroshi to go back over his autopsy findings, maybe even send a sample out for more extensive testing, but I'm not holding my breath."

Gavin nodded. "All right. You'd better get downtown."

———

Gavin watched Ike and Pete leave the pit and head off to their second shooting location. When he turned to go back to his office he couldn't help but notice the handful of glances shooting his way.

Detectives in every corner of the pit looking and whispering.

He rolled his eyes at no one in particular and marched to his office with one question burning a hole in his gut. How the hell long was it going to take before he and Gerri were no longer the talk of the whole damn station?

It had been nearly two months since Gerri had transferred to the Violent Crimes division, and yet the salacious rumors continued to circulate.

He ignored the stares and entered his office with a good mind to slam the door for effect. But instead, he left it open and took a seat behind his desk. He had more important things to focus on than the childish gossip that often swept the precinct's fourth floor. And he especially didn't want to hear it if he was the topic.

He got back to work, concentrating on the paperwork in front of him, when a knock sounded at his open office door. A casual glance up had him quickly getting to his feet.

"Captain Brewster."

Bright, smiling blue eyes greeted him from beneath a shock of almost white hair, but Gavin still remembered the light brown it used to be. Tom Brewster was a bear of a man. Bulky, grizzly, and very nearly as wild. But he was a good cop, and he'd had a hand in teaching Gavin everything he knew about the job. He also happened to be head of the entire Detectives Division, and as such, was Gavin's commanding officer.

Brewster walked in without an invitation and closed the door behind him.

"Gavin, we need to talk."

Was it the words themselves, or the serious tone with which they were spoken that had Gavin's stomach tightening?

"Certainly, sir."

"Now, don't start with the sir crap! It's just you and me in here right now."

Brewster sat down, and Gavin did the same, wondering what fresh hell was about to ignite.

"All right. What's going on, Tom?"

"I guess I need to ask you that same question." Brewster stared him in the eyes. "Rumor has it you're sleeping with a subordinate. Please tell me I don't have to spank your ass like a just-cleared-for-duty rookie."

Gavin flopped back in his desk chair and shook his head.

The damn rumor mill.

"Ah... I don't hear you denying it."

"That's because there's nothing to deny, Tom. I'm not sleeping with a subordinate."

"Rumors start somewhere. Where'd this one come from?"

Gavin sighed. "Are you interested in the salacious details of the rumor, or do you want to hear the truth?"

"Truth. Always."

"All right." Gavin leaned forward and folded his hands together on top of the desk and looked his boss in the eyes. "The short version is that I did develop feelings for one of my female detectives. Actually... she developed feelings for me. Her mistake was in letting me know that. Once she did..."

He paused and shook his head like he still couldn't believe it. Because frankly, he couldn't.

"The fact that someone like me actually had a chance with someone like her? Let's just say it was flattering as hell. And the longer the flirtation went on, the more I realized that I wasn't simply flattered. But suffice it to say that we talked about our situation for months. And when we finally got to a point where we wanted to pursue a relationship, we discussed our options. Transfer was the solution. So, she ended up leaving Homicide for Violent Crimes. End of story."

He spread his hands apart as if to say, 'that's that.'

"I'm sure it's not as exciting as the rumors."

Tom Brewster stared at him.

"So, Detective Miller is the subordinate in question then?"

"She is."

"Okay." Brewster nodded, still looking Gavin in the eyes. Then he glanced nonchalantly around the office.

"And you two never knocked boots before she transferred, right?"

Gavin didn't know whether to be amused at the older guy using the slang euphemism, or angry at being called out. He looked away, not sure how to answer.

"Look, I'm not trying to piss in your soup, Gavin, and I don't want to pry into your sex life either. I'm just trying to help cover your ass here."

"I get that, Tom."

"The good thing is that you did right in the end. Your girl was willing to transfer out to protect your position. That's stand up. The rumor mill can churn all it wants to, but the bottom line is you two did the right thing without jeopardizing either of your careers."

He leaned in and tapped the desk.

"There. This conversation had to happen, and now it's on the record. Consider yourself reprimanded."

"That's it?"

"That's it. The gossip spread around this floor like lightning, so I had to address it before it went up any further. I don't want anyone accusing me of not supervising the lieutenants running my detectives division. Also, you're a good lieutenant, Gavin. And I didn't want this minor indiscretion to trip you up."

Blessed relief washed in like a flood, and Gavin smiled.

"Thanks for having my back, Tom. I struggled with this. A lot."

Brewster studied him for a moment and then grinned.

"I'll be damned. You're happy."

"What?"

"This woman makes you happy."

Gavin laughed and looked away. How was he supposed to respond to that? He couldn't deny it.

Brewster stood, still smiling. "It looks good on you, old friend."

Gavin tried to swallow the embarrassment as he stood too.

"Thanks."

The captain turned and left his office, and Gavin chuckled to himself and got back to work.

———

When Isaac and Pete pulled up outside the bar, there were several marked cruisers and two ambulances already in the parking lot. They crossed the police tape and Isaac glanced around at the carnage. The scene was eerily similar to the one they'd left only a couple of hours ago at the bowling alley.

Two uniformed cops were holding what he correctly assumed were the bar's patrons in one corner of the parking lot, and Isaac saw the paramedics working on another two who were clearly wounded.

They approached the bar's entrance, and a CSU tech was waiting for them there.

"It's pretty tight quarters inside, Detective. We were waiting for you guys to have a look before we start collecting evidence."

Isaac gave her a curt nod. "Understood."

They both pulled on a pair of latex gloves and stepped inside.

The smell of stale beer and cigarettes smacked him in the face, and Isaac recoiled from the nauseatingly familiar scent.

The scene wasn't much better. War zone was the phrase that jumped immediately to mind.

There were three dead bodies inside — two male, one female — and the entire place had been shot up.

"Good God," Pete whispered, looking around at the damage.

"If this is the same shooter from the bowling alley, he is really racking up the bodies."

"You know, it's almost like he's on some kind of video game shoot 'em up rampage."

Isaac glanced at Pete and nodded.

"That's not a bad theory, Pete. Could be some gamer who's snapped and suddenly thinks he's inside Fortnite or Call of Duty or something."

A slow grin settled on Pete's face.

"Are you a secret gamer, Ike?"

"What?"

"I'm just surprised you know the names of those games is all."

Isaac turned and smirked at him.

"You do realize I'm only eight years older than you, right? I'm not completely ancient."

Pete chuckled, and Isaac stepped carefully closer to the bar area. Since the CSU techs hadn't begun yet, he wanted to disturb the scene as little as possible. His gaze scanned every inch of the small space.

He pointed to a camera above the bar and looked at Pete.

"Make sure we get all surveillance footage to the IT department. We have got to identify our shooter. Hopefully before he has a chance to add to his body count."

Pete nodded. "I'll see to it."

"All right. Let's go interview witnesses."

They carefully exited the bar and gave CSU the go-ahead. Then they got busy talking to witnesses. And one-by-one, they all had a similar story to tell.

"The gun was golden. With, like... a white handle. But not just white. It was like jewelry white. Like, what's that stuff called? Mother of pearl? Like that!"

"The shooter? Well, he was a man. Definitely a man."

"No, he was a white guy. I'm pretty sure. Or maybe Latinx. I think?"

"Definitely a tall man!"

"Heavy. And short!"

"I'm afraid I didn't really see him. But the gun was golden! With like... ivory grips."

By the time they'd spoken to each of them, Isaac was fighting off a headache. He sat behind the wheel of the car, rubbing his temples.

"I just don't get it." Pete sounded as frustrated as Isaac felt. "How can you get such a detailed look at the gun in someone's hand, but not be able to tell what the person holding the gun looks like?"

"I don't know."

"It doesn't make any sense! It's probably not even humanly possible. It's not like the shooter was at point blank range. The gun wasn't directly in their faces. So how'd they get such a detailed look at it, but not the guy holding it?"

"I don't know, Pete."

Isaac started the car and headed back to the station.

"Hopefully, the camera footage from the bar will give us a little more to go on. Although, I admit, it does all seem more than a little abnormal."

"Doesn't it though?"

Isaac drove on, wondering about the odd case, and what it all meant.

———

Sidney left Hope House and slid behind the steering wheel of her car, and dialed the number for the mysterious man named Ronan O'Dwyer. The forger that Ike had sent her to.

It rang only once before it was answered by the now familiar Irish brogue.

"Yeah?"

"Is this Ronan?" She had to be sure.

"Who's asking?"

"This is Sid."

"Ah. Sid the social worker, is it? I wondered if I'd be hearing from ya again. I trust ya were pleased with me skills then?"

"Yes. It worked out very well."

"And now yer back fer more. Well, what can I do fer ya, Sid?"

"I need a drivers license, plus birth certificates for a woman and a young girl."

"No passports this time?"

"No. This one has chosen a remote corner of this great nation instead."

There was a soft chuckle from him.

"Well then, you're looking at an even $500. A hundred fer the license, one fifty each fer the two documents. Another hundred fer me time and labor. Sound fair?"

"Perfectly fair. And if you rush it, I'll double it."

An offer she never would've made if she hadn't discussed it with Beth first. But the woman was desperate to get away as quickly as possible.

"Now, now. Ya don't want sloppy work, do ya, Sid?"

"Of course not. But time is of the essence on my end. For more reasons than one."

A brief pause sat between them.

"Need to get this one to safety quickly then?"

"Something like that."

"All right. I'll see what I can do. Ya have digital pictures fer me?"

"Yes, and all the pertinent information."

"Good girl. Remembered the rules this time. Ya know what to do with it then. I'll contact ya in 24 hours with a meetin' place."

"Thanks, Ronan. I appreciate it."

"I appreciate the business, Sid the social worker."

The line went dead, and Sidney texted the pictures and information to Ronan's number. Then she started the car and headed for home.

5

*P*ete was pushing it. He and Ike had chased their tails at work the whole rest of the day after the second shooting — running down the three new victims, questioning their known associates, putting the heat on the IT department to put a rush on things. But no matter what they did, the day had ended with a lot more questions than answers.

His brain was so fried by the time he clocked out half an hour early. Then he battled rush hour traffic to make it back downtown by 5:45 for the meeting his mother had set up to look into getting Mateo's guardianship transferred.

He hated being late for anything, but the traffic just would not cooperate. A couple of times he thought about turning on the police light he kept in his car, but even more than being late, he hated the thought of abusing his power.

When he finally got to the law building it took him another five minutes to find parking. Then he rushed inside the lobby and came face-to-face with his mother and his old friend and attorney, Steven Sanchez.

"Hey! I'm so sorry. I know I'm cutting it close, but the traffic was horrendous." Pete greeted his friend with a fist bump and kissed his mother on the cheek.

"No, it's okay, man. Take a breath. My friend is running about five minutes behind too, so you're not late."

He'd known Steven since high school and was grateful his old soccer buddy now provided free and low cost legal aid for the local Latinx community.

"Oh, good. Hey, listen, thanks again for doing this, Steven. We really appreciate the introduction."

"It's no problem. I'm only sorry that I couldn't handle it for you myself. But family law is not my area of expertise."

Steven's cellphone buzzed and he pulled it from his pocket and read a text.

"Okay, she's ready. Let's head up."

Steven gestured to the elevator, and Pete lead his mother inside. They got off on the fifth floor and were ushered into a large, impressive office where a very pretty Latina woman in a sharp and flattering business suit greeted them with a warm smile.

"Marisol Peña," Steven began the introductions, "this is my good friend, Detective Pete Vega, and his mother, Señora Julieta Vega. This is Marisol Peña, one of the best family law attorneys in the city."

"Thank you for the flattery, Steven, but we don't need the exaggeration."

She reached out and Pete met her assessing gaze and shook her hand.

"Just stating the facts, counselor," Steven smiled at her.

After shaking hands with Julieta, Marisol waved them all over to a large round table in the corner of her office. The grand view of the city from the picture window made the office seem palatial.

Pete took a seat between his mom and Steven.

"Can I offer anyone some water or coffee?" Marisol said as she sat down on the opposite side of the table.

"No, thank you."

Pete and Julieta responded in unison.

Marisol laced her fingers together on top of the table and glanced around at them.

"So. Steven's told me a little bit about your situation, but I'd like to hear it from you. What can I help you with?"

Pete took a deep breath and exchanged a look with his mom.

"Well, we were hoping that you could walk us through the steps of getting my nephew's guardianship transferred from my mother over to me. We have no idea what all that entails, or how difficult a process it might be. Whether or not we'd need Mateo's mother's input..."

He spread his hands wide and let that sentence dangle.

"Okay. Well, first things first," Marisol nodded and looked at Julieta. "Tell me how you came to have guardianship of your grandson, Señora Vega."

"Please, call me Julieta."

"All right, Julieta," Marisol smiled at her.

"My daughter, Paulina... she was convicted of armed robbery and 2nd degree murder."

"Oh, I'm sorry to hear that."

"Yes," Julieta sighed. "We all are."

"How old is the child?"

"He'll be 14 in September. But before she was sentenced, Paulina named me Mateo's legal guardian."

"How much time did she get?" Marisol looked back and forth between them all, and began taking notes on a yellow legal pad.

"Fifteen to twenty," Pete responded.

"And who was your family legal counsel at that time?"

Pete and Julieta both looked to Steven, who quietly cleared his throat.

"Well, you know I volunteer at Community Legal Aid," Steven said.

"Right." Marisol nodded.

"So, I handled all the guardianship paperwork back then since

I was also Paulina's legal counsel during her trial. But now, I feel it's best that they have an actual family law attorney going forward."

"I see. Okay." Marisol nodded again and turned back to Julieta. "And are you no longer able to properly house your grandson, or make decisions for his care?"

"Well, no." Julieta's tone was slightly confused, and she began twisting her fingers. "We all live in the same house anyway. That's not the issue. We just feel it would be better for Mateo if Pedro were made his legal guardian instead of me. He needs a man's presence in his life."

Marisol studied them, and Pete could see the confusion all over her face. She shifted in her chair and lifted a hand as she spoke.

"You all reside in the same home?"

"Yes." Pete nodded with the word, for emphasis.

"Then he already has a male presence in his life, correct?"

"Yes, but you see... we want to do this for legal reasons. So that it's documented that Mateo belongs with me."

"But is there some reason for the switch?" Marisol asked again. "Here's the thing... a family court judge will be very reluctant to make a switch like this if the current arrangement is working. And it sounds as though yours is. As long as the child is being well cared for, there would have to be a compelling reason for the change in guardianship."

"A compelling reason?" Pete repeated.

"Yes. Something like diminished capacity on Julieta's part. Say, for instance, if she'd had a stroke or something like that, and could no longer make decisions for Mateo's welfare. That sort of thing."

Pete flopped back in his chair, deflated. Like she'd reached out and stuck a straight pin into his balloon. He wanted to do this for Mateo. So that the kid knew without a doubt that his place was with Pete, no matter what. He just wanted to give the kid some peace of mind. Now that couldn't happen.

He was about to thank Ms. Peña for her time, but Julieta spoke up first.

"We have a compelling reason."

Her voice was small. Her accent was heavy.

Pete glanced over at her.

"We do?"

"What is it, Julieta?"

Julieta looked up from her folded hands and looked Marisol in the eyes.

"My cancer is back. Dr. Linden says it's stage three."

Pete stared at his mother.

All air left the room.

Her words were a giant vacuum that sucked everything out.

His lungs wouldn't work.

He struggled to take a breath.

"*Mamá, por qué dirías tal cosa?*" Why would you say such a thing? Why was she doing this?

"Pretense is never a good strategy, *mamá*."

Even as the words left his mouth, he knew the truth.

He could see it in her eyes as she looked at him.

"It's not a pretense or a strategy, *mijo. Es verdad.*" It's true.

"What? Since when?"

His voice had gone up an octave, but he couldn't seem to bring it down.

His chest felt tight.

Was it getting warm in the room?

"Since my recent check up."

"No." Pete shook his head. "No, you came home from that appointment and told me everything was fine, *mamá*! Y-you've been doing great these last few years."

Julieta put her hand on top of his.

"*Lo siento, mijo.*" I'm sorry, my son. "I wasn't trying to keep things from you. Two days ago the doctor's office called and wanted me to come in to discuss the results of my bloodwork."

"Two days ago?"

"Yes."

"That's when you called Steven and asked him to get moving on this guardianship transfer. You knew then and you didn't tell me?"

"Pedro." Julieta patted his hand. "This doesn't mean I'm dying. It only means that we should make sure things are in order. Right? That's why I called Steven."

Pete turned away from her and stared out the window at the city.

This wasn't happening. Was it?

Across from him, Marisol quietly cleared her throat.

"I'm so sorry about your diagnosis, Julieta."

"Me too," Steven spoke up. "But hey. If anyone can beat this, it's you."

Pete heard their conversation like he was under water, the voices muffled and murky.

His mother patted his hand once more. Pete flipped his hand over and took hers in his, lightly squeezing it.

"Well, this information certainly changes things," Marisol was saying. "Your diagnosis is a compelling enough reason to seek a transfer of guardianship for your grandson. And since the child's mother is in prison for fifteen to twenty years, I'm assuming she's already been stripped of her parental rights?"

Still unable to rejoin the conversation just then, Pete assumed that question had been meant for Steven.

"Yes, she has," Steven answered, placing a strong hand on Pete's shoulder.

Pete appreciated the support, but his gaze stayed on the city and he continued to hold his mom's hand.

"Good. That means we don't actually have to notify her of this transfer. She has no authority to make decisions on Mateo's welfare. If she should find out about the transfer she *could* petition the court as an interested party, but I'd be surprised if she bothered to do so."

"So you will help us?" Julieta asked, sounding hopeful.

"I'll get started on the paperwork first thing in the morning."

Pete heard his mother sigh in relief and lightly squeezed her hand again.

"You should know that the court will be looking at you very closely, Detective."

At that, Pete finally looked up and made an effort to rejoin the conversation.

"What do you mean?"

"Well, family courts tend to be very serious about who they're placing children with. Any surprises I should know about going in?"

Puzzled, he shook his head. "Surprises?"

Marisol met his gaze.

"DUIs? Restraining orders or physical rows with old girlfriends? Spots on your record at work? Anything that might not make you look like the best guardian candidate for your nephew?"

"No. There's nothing."

Marisol nodded. "Okay. I'll be in touch once the paperwork is filed. Once it is, these things usually take about a month, barring any roadblocks. And since you all reside in the same home already, it should be a fairly smooth process."

"And about my sister? If she did petition the court, could she stop the process?"

"I doubt it." Marisol shook her head. "Unless she had a very good reason why you shouldn't be granted guardianship, the most she could do is stall us. At any rate, I wouldn't worry too much about that."

They shook Marisol's hand and left the office. Down in the lobby again, Pete and Julieta said goodbye to Steven. Then Pete walked his mom to her car in silence.

"*Mijo?* Are you angry with me?"

Pete sighed and opened her door. "No, *mamá*. I just feel blind-sided is all."

She laid her palm against his cheek.

"I'm sorry. That was not my intention."

"I know. Listen, you be careful driving home, okay?"

"Aren't you coming home too?"

"Yes. I'll be right behind you. But I parked around the corner. Just drive safe. I'll see you at home."

"All right."

He waited until she'd gotten in and strapped on her seatbelt. Then he turned and walked slowly back to his car, his thoughts jumbled in a fog.

6

*S*he enjoyed cooking, but it was rare that Emily Taylor spent hours slaving away in the kitchen. Most nights she just popped one of those healthy frozen dinners into the microwave after putting in a twelve or thirteen hour day at her graphic design business. But not so tonight. Tonight was special.

Tonight, she'd rushed through work, showered and primped, and then spent quality time with her stove making dinner for Special Agent Emmett Fox.

It was, officially, only their third date, and she wanted it to be both fun and casual. So far, so good.

She watched him now, devouring the baked pork chops, mashed potatoes, fried apples and green beans. His enthusiastic appetite made her smile.

"Mmm. Wow." Emmett sat back in his chair and stared at his empty plate. "That was the most delicious home cooked meal I've had in a long time."

"Was it now?"

Emmett looked at her with a sheepish grin.

"Actually, it was the first home cooked meal I've had since..."

He paused, and Emily could actually see his mind working.

"Since...?" she prodded.

"Hmm. It's been so long I don't even remember. How sad is that?"

Emily giggled. "That's pretty sad. There's plenty more if you'd like seconds."

"You mean thirds."

"I was trying to be polite."

Emmett laughed out loud, and Emily smiled.

"It's okay. I think we both know that I've eaten like a pig tonight. I'll own that. You can say it."

"Well, I will happily send the leftovers home with you if you'd like."

"Really? You wouldn't mind?"

"Not at all. Do you cook?"

"Not exactly. I mean, I know how to make a few things. Grilled cheese. And, um... I can boil spaghetti and open up a jar of sauce." He paused again and shifted in his seat. "Well, I know how to heat things up in the microwave. Frozen dinners and such. And honestly, with the crazy hours I've been putting in lately, that's about all I typically have time for. I had to practically bribe a couple of fellow agents in order to get the evening off to be here with you tonight."

"Seriously?"

Emily could hear the mild shock in her own voice, but she couldn't help it.

"Well, that might be a small exaggeration, but it's not far off."

"Oh, that sounds like a serious problem, Agent Fox."

"It does, doesn't it?"

"Indeed. You know, I think, for the sake of your good health, we should probably plan on one of these home cooked meals together at least once or twice a week."

She was pushing hard, and she knew it. But she didn't give a damn, she really liked this guy. She wanted so badly for this to work out, and if the way to this particular man's heart was through his stomach, she would happily cook for him all the time if it would seal the deal.

"Ooh. Once or twice a week? You really think the problem is that serious?"

"I do."

"Hmm. You could be right. And I will admit, the thought of a meal like this even once a week sounds like heaven. But I don't think I could let you feed me on a regular basis like that. I would feel bad. I don't want you to think of me as charity."

"You're joking, right?"

"What?"

"Charity?"

"Well..."

"I could never view cooking dinner for you as charity."

"No?"

"No."

"Then how would you see it, Ms. Taylor?"

"As a date. A standing, weekly date with a charming, hand-some man."

Emmett looked pleasantly shocked.

"Charming and handsome, huh? Can't deny I'm flattered to hear you think so."

"Oh, please. I'm sure it's not the first time you've had a woman call you both."

"It's the first time Emily Taylor has ever called me either. And *that* makes this a great night."

Emily smiled at him and stood to gather their plates. Emmett stood and helped her clear the table. When they'd finished, she poured them each another glass of wine and then led him over to the couch.

She slipped off her shoes and pulled her legs up beneath her, and Emmett sat back beside her.

"So, tell me all about yourself, Agent Fox."

"I will only do that if you stop calling me Agent Fox. I get enough of it at work. Here with you, I'm just Emmett."

"Okay, but it works both ways. From now on, no more Agent Fox and Ms. Taylor. When we're together, we're just Emmett and Emily."

"Well, now... that almost sounds like a couple that's meant to be together, doesn't it?"

"It does at that."

He smiled at her, and Emily felt her belly ripple. He was seriously crush-worthy with his liquid brown eyes, and strong jaw, and that mat of dark curly hair she just wanted to run her fingers through. He had a soft olive tint to his skin and an easy smile that offset the seriousness of his brow.

"At least, it would if one half of that couple wasn't such a workaholic."

"Excuse me? This coming from the woman who routinely works twelve hours every day?"

"Yes, but I'm trying to get a new small business off the ground. I have an excuse."

"Oh, I see. I guess trying to put away bad guys isn't a good enough excuse?"

Emily smiled and sipped her wine, never taking her eyes off his.

"I guess that's a good excuse. I'll let you use it this time anyway."

"Thank you. I so appreciate it."

"So tell me more about you."

"What would you like to know?"

"Mmm. Well, I know you were born in upstate New York and raised in Boulder, Colorado."

"Correct."

"Are your parents from there?"

"Not originally. My mom is Mexican American."

"Really?"

"Yep. She grew up in Laredo, Texas, right on the boarder. And as a kid we used to spend a few weeks every summer down in Laredo visiting her family. Occasionally we even went to Monterrey, Mexico to see my great-grandparents."

"Wow. What was that like?"

"Colorful. That's how I always think of Mexico. You remember that moment when Dorothy stepped out out of the house after the tornado landed her in Oz?"

"The explosion of color?"

"Exactly. That's Mexico to me."

Emily smiled at his description.

"What about your dad?"

"My dad was born and raised in Syracuse, New York. But after medical school he took a job at Boulder Community Hospital. Met my mom there on a blind date and the rest is history."

"And here you are."

"And here I am."

"You know, I always wonder about couples who met on a blind date. It sounds so random, yet sometimes it apparently works out."

Emmett nodded. "It sure worked out for them. They're still together, still embarrassing me in public."

Emily laughed, and he smiled at her.

"It's a good point though. That blind dates are so random."

"Right?" Emily nodded. "Like, I wonder what percentage of blind dates actually result in marriage? Especially versus other forms of random meetings."

"I don't know. But our meeting was definitely random."

"You think?"

"Heck yes. I mean, I catch a random kidnapping case and it happens to be your brother's girlfriend. We end that case, and a few months later, your brother comes to me with another case he needs help with. And he said he came to me because I took his psychic abilities at face value during our first meeting."

Emmett paused and shrugged a shoulder, and Emily suddenly got the feeling that he both liked and respected her big brother.

"So, basically... if I hadn't been cool about his abilities, if I'd ridiculed him for it or acted like a jerk about them, you and I never would've met. 'Cause he wouldn't have come to me for that second case. And if he hadn't come to me for help with that case, I never would've had the occasion to go to his house the night we met."

A slow smile spread over Emily's face. "So we could almost say it was fate."

"We could."

"Kismet?"

"I think it applies."

"Destiny?"

Emmett sucked in a breath, releasing a low whistling sound.

"That's a serious word, but... yes."

"Wow. Heavy."

"It certainly is. Kind of makes that weekly dinner thing sound like a must, doesn't it?"

"Well, at this point I'd be afraid not to. I mean, if it's our *destiny!*"

They laughed and then stared into each other's eyes for a long moment. Emmett leaned in, and Emily let him capture her lips with his. She closed her eyes and enjoyed the fireworks display going off in her head.

"So, next Monday good for you?" Her voice was breathy, and her lips felt plump from the kiss.

"For a home cooked meal? Yes. But case-permitting, I really hope to see you before that too."

He kissed her again, making Emily's head spin.

"Yes, please. And Emmett?"

She pulled herself away from his lips and looked into his eyes. "Yes?"

"Would you like to be my plus one for Ike and Sidney's wedding?"

"I would like that very much."

7

*Q*uestions, questions, questions.

Isaac had nothing but questions clouding his brain. Two separate cases full of nothing but questions. First, the suspicious death of a wealthy businessman, young and healthy, who seemed convinced that he'd die of a long-standing family curse, supposedly just like his father, his grandfather, and his great-grandfather. Not to mention a few uncles and male cousins along the way. It was completely ridiculous, and Isaac had no clue where to begin.

Then there was the strange shooting case. Two locations presumably targeted by the same man. He and Pete got absolutely nowhere on that. The second shooting had left them in even deeper — more bodies, more headaches — with still nowhere to begin. No leads, no nothing. And now, all Isaac wanted was to put the day behind him, get home to Sidney and lose himself inside her.

He walked into the house dragging a chain of frustration, aggravation, and stress behind him.

"Meow."

"Meow to you too, Mr. Hitchcock."

He bent over to give the fluffy cat a quick scratch. Then he followed his nose to the kitchen where Sidney had just taken a roasting pan out of the oven and shut it off.

She looked up and smiled at him.

"Hey, baby."

"Hey."

She moved in for a kiss, but Isaac ducked down and swooped her off her feet.

"Whoop! Isaac?"

He grinned at her laughter, but he kept moving. A man on a sudden, unstoppable mission.

He carried her back to the bedroom and set her down on the bed, capturing her mouth with his own. The kiss was urgent and fevered, and Isaac felt a freight train of longing power through him.

Hands groped and worked.

Clothing fell away.

He wasted not a single second on greetings or conversation. His lips and tongue moved over her silky skin, drinking in the scent of her as his hands squeezed and kneaded soft flesh.

Her legs closed around his waist.

"Isaac."

His name dropped from her lips, whispered breathlessly, as though in shock. The sound of it spurred his desire, revving up the already dire need within him. He entered her with one long, smooth thrust.

He began to move, setting a burning, frenzied pace. Conscious thought was gone. All that remained was need.

He needed this.

He needed her.

He needed the sweet oblivion that he could only find when he was inside her.

"Isaac!"

This time his name was a shout, and he kissed her, absorbing her moans of ecstasy as her body trembled beneath him. One final thrust and he lost himself completely, dragged over the edge by the same freight train of longing that had launched this liaison.

He collapsed on top of her, his face buried in her mountain of curls, his senses surrounded by the gingered honeysuckle scent of her perfume.

God, he loved that smell. The smell of her. His Sidney.

Knowing that he must be crushing her, he pulled out of her and rolled onto his back and stared up at the ceiling.

"How is it that you always take me through the stratosphere, darlin'?" His words were huffed out between panting breaths. "I mean... I feel like this is supposed to be getting old, right? Isn't that what couples supposedly complain about all the time? The sex becomes routine?"

Sidney laughed, and Isaac grinned at the sound of it.

"The sex is never going to become routine with you and me, baby."

"No?"

"Not a chance. Want to know why?"

"Yes, please."

"Because it's all still so new to you. Sex. Touching someone without pain. Allowing me to touch you. And then there's me. I'm still not used to having a man be so sweet and giving in bed. You're such an unselfish lover, Ike."

"That's a good thing?"

"That's an amazing thing. So sex between us is never going to become routine."

"That is so good to know." He rolled over and kissed her, gently sucking on her tongue for a few seconds. Then he tickled her, just because he could.

Sidney giggled and pushed his hands away. Then she sat up, running a hand through her mass of curls.

"So how was your day after our lunch? I would've asked

sooner, but I didn't get a chance. I was too busy letting you carry me off to bed."

Isaac laughed and sat up next to her, propping up the pillows behind him.

"Sorry. Guess I did kinda roll up in here hot and ready, didn't I?"

"You certainly did. Not that I'm complaining, mind you."

Isaac sighed and took her hand, playing with her fingers.

"My day was long and weird. Before I left to meet you at the courthouse to get our marriage license, Pete and I were working on this case where the victim and all of his family seem to believe wholeheartedly in this supposed family curse that makes all the men in the family die at a young age."

"Really?"

"Yeah. I guess none of them live to see forty."

"Wow. That is really young. But a curse?"

"That's what they believe. But the widow of this guy is insisting that the curse isn't real and that someone killed her husband."

"But who supposedly set this curse?"

"Oh, that's where it gets real believable. A witch."

"A witch?"

"A witch. Apparently, back when this guy's great-grandfather was a teenager, someone in the family pissed off a witch somehow, and she cursed all the males of the family."

"Okay."

"Then after our lunch, that call I had to go on?"

"Yes. A shooting in broad daylight."

"Right. Well, now there are two shootings in two different locations. We've got five dead, four wounded, and zero suspects."

"Oh, my God. Really?"

Isaac nodded. "None of the witnesses can tell us a single concrete thing about the shooter, but most of them give a very detailed description of the gun the shooter used. Crazy."

"Wait. They describe the gun?"

"Yeah. An ornate gold-plated Colt .45 with ivory grips. Polished so that it gleams in the sunlight." Isaac raised a jazz hand on that last part, for emphasis.

"They got that specific a look at the gun, but not at the man holding it?"

"Now you understand my frustration."

"That sounds impossible."

Isaac snorted. "Sounds like complete and utter horse shit. And Pete and I chased our tails all afternoon long on this thing, interviewing witnesses and known associates. None of the victims are connected in any way. We just hit a big brick wall. So coming in here and grabbing you and losing myself inside you for a while was exactly what I needed tonight."

"I'm sorry you had such a frustrating day." Sidney ran a hand over his face, and Isaac leaned into it.

"You made it better." He smiled at her.

"Would you like dinner now that you've already had dessert?"

"Only if we can eat it here, in bed. I don't really want to move."

"That can absolutely be arranged. I made a beef roast with potatoes and carrots. Some mustard greens."

"That sounds great."

"I'll go make us plates and get the tray."

She climbed out of bed, and Isaac couldn't resist reaching over and giving her firm ass a small pinch.

Sidney swatted his hand away and smiled at him. Then she went into the bathroom.

Isaac spread out in the bed and closed his eyes. He was on his way to dozing off when Sidney emerged from the bathroom wearing a short silk robe and headed for the kitchen.

With a sigh, Isaac sat up on the edge of the bed. The shooting and the family curse case tried to sneak their way back in, but he shut them down. He got up and pulled his underwear back on. Then he left the bedroom in search of his woman.

In the kitchen, Sidney had loaded up a serving tray with two plates of food.

"You said you didn't want to move."

"I didn't. But I didn't want you to have to carry all this back to the bedroom by yourself either." He picked up the loaded tray. "I got this. You grab drinks and forks."

Once back in the bedroom, they climbed into bed and settled in for their meal.

"Mmm. This is delicious, Sid."

"Thanks. I'm glad you like it."

Isaac grunted and shoveled in another bite.

"Hey, are you going to be able to swing by the hotel tomorrow for brunch with my family?"

Isaac nodded. "I'm going to try. What time are you doing that again?"

"Well, their plane gets in early. Like 8:20 or something, I think. So, Simon and I are supposed to meet them at ten."

"Simon's driving up for this?"

He knew that Sidney's older brother was only a few hours away now that he was stationed down at Wright-Patt Air Force Base in Dayton, but for some reason, the early hour struck him.

"Well, yeah. He hasn't seen them in years either."

"He'll have to get on the road around six in the morning to make it by ten."

"Actually, he's already on his way."

"Oh, he is?"

"He called just before you got home. Said he was driving up and checking in at the hotel tonight."

"Well, that's smart, I guess. No sense in rushing in the morning if you don't have to."

"Yeah. I'm excited to see them."

"Now, who all's coming again?"

"My Aunt Bobbie and Uncle Frank, and their daughters, Erika and Tameka. And Tameka is bringing her husband, Jamal, and their little boy, Jabari."

"And he's the one who's going to be the bell ringer in our wedding?"

"Right. It's so weird for me to think of Tameka as married now, with a child. The last time I saw them, she'd just had her little boy, but she and Jamal weren't even thinking about marriage. I'd only met him a couple of times at that point. God, I've missed so much with all of them."

She suddenly sounded sad. But then she perked right back up.

"And I can't wait for you to meet them. I've been telling them all about how wonderful you are."

Isaac rolled his eyes and smiled at her.

"Hmm. I'm sure that went over well."

"Isaac..."

He could hear it in her voice. She already knew what he was thinking.

"It's not that I don't want to meet your family, darlin'. You know I do."

"I know. You're not crazy about meeting any new people, and the whole shaking hands thing, and how much do we tell them. I get it. But I don't want you to worry about any of that, okay? I'll take care of it. I promise."

He leaned in and kissed her lips. What else was there to say? His huge freakdom was his issue, not hers. He would suck it up and deal with it.

"There's something else I should probably tell you."

Her voice held a notable measure of dread.

"Why don't I like the sound of that?"

Sidney sighed, clearly stalling.

He reached out and lightly touched her cheek, blatantly using his abilities to check in on her.

Dead cold danger.

It hit his gut like a sledgehammer.

It was a vibe that encircled her.

"Sidney?"

"When I was at Hope House today, Beth, one of the residents, she came in crying and frantic because the cops still can't locate her abusive boyfriend, and yet he keeps sending her threatening texts and notes. And today she begged me to help her get away."

"Okaaay."

Isaac drew out the word, waiting for more. He knew there was more.

"She wants to get away as quickly as possible. This week."

"And you told her you'd help. Even though you've got a million things to do seeing as it's the week of our wedding."

"I had no choice, baby. She didn't want to wait for me to get back from our honeymoon. And when she told me about this guy I really wanted to help her. He's not only been beating Beth, he's also been molesting Kylee, her little girl."

Isaac sighed.

"Has she told the cops about the threatening texts? We can trace those, you know?"

"She has. But they keep telling her that the phone he's texting from must be a burner. They can't trace it."

"If this interferes with our wedding or our honeymoon in any way..."

"It won't. I promise."

Isaac took a last bite of his dinner and wondered if he should tell her about the danger he felt. It was just like when they'd first met. That aura of danger he'd felt around her back then. Back when she was being stalked by both an evil drug lord and her abusive, murdering former husband, Damien Jarvis.

"Now, about another pressing wedding matter..."

"Okay, I don't like the sound of that either." He stared at her and waited for the boom. "What is it?"

"Just a question."

"Yeah?"

"Where are we going on our honeymoon?"

Isaac laughed out loud, forgetting about the danger for the moment.

"How many times are you going to ask me that?"

"I don't know. Just until you finally tell me."

"Well, I'm not going to tell you, Sid."

"Isaac, some on! I need to know what to pack."

"I told you what to pack…"

"…a bathing suit!" they said in unison.

Isaac grinned. "See? You do know what to pack."

He climbed out of bed and gathered up the remnants of their dinner onto the tray and then carried it back out to the kitchen, still smiling. He scraped the plates and loaded up the dishwasher. Then he went back to the bedroom.

And stopped short the second he stepped inside.

Sidney was sprawled seductively across the bed, completely naked.

His breath hitched in his throat.

His heart stalled in his chest.

His dick twitched in his shorts.

"Are you sure you don't want to tell me where we're honeymooning?"

Isaac stepped further into the room, and stepped out of his underwear.

"Yep. I'm sure."

"Oh, please? Isn't there anything I can do to change your mind?"

Slowly, he sank a knee onto the foot of the bed and began to crawl toward her.

"Nope."

He kissed the inside of her knee and moved steadily up, placing another soft kiss on the inside of her thigh.

"Now you're just being mean."

"Let me make it up to you."

He settled between her legs and gave her a different kind of kiss.

8

"You look nervous, Sid."

Sidney moved her shoulders around and straightened her pink silk top, smoothed out the pink and burgundy skirt of her outfit and looked herself over in the hotel mirror once more. She shot a frustrated glance at her brother's reflection.

"I am a little nervous. But I'm also excited. Aren't you excited, Simon? I mean, I haven't seen Aunt Bobbie in like, four years! It's been longer for you. And this is the first time that we'll all be together since..."

She paused and tried to remember how long.

The sharp sting of sadness hit her heart when she did.

"Well, since that first Christmas right after mom died."

Her fingers went immediately to the dainty, delicate gold necklace that she always wore. The one that had been her mothers.

"That's a big deal, you know?"

Simon smiled at her and nodded.

"Yes, it is."

Then he sat down on the edge of the hotel bed to put on his socks and shoes.

"So where is Ike? Is he coming this morning?"

Sidney sighed and leaned gingerly against the edge of the table in front of the mirror.

"He's going to try to, but he's working."

"Oh. He didn't take the week off like you did?"

"No, he couldn't. It was either work the week of the wedding, or only take one week for our honeymoon."

"Ah. Good choice."

"We thought so. Although he flat out refuses to tell me where we're going for the honeymoon. I knew I shouldn't have agreed to let him plan it by himself. He won't even give me a hint. I even tried checking the browsing history on our computer at home, hoping for a clue, but there's nothing. He's being very sneaky."

Simon chuckled, which slightly annoyed her.

"Would you relax and let the man surprise you? He's gone to a lot of trouble to make your honeymoon trip a special one. Don't ruin it."

Sidney stared at her brother with wide eyes and her mouth gaping open. She pointed a finger at him.

"You know something!"

Simon looked at her and said nothing as he stepped into his shoes.

"Simon? What do you know?"

"I know that you will get no information about it from me."

"Oh, come on!"

"No, Sid. Stop. I am not telling you anything. Now, just trust me... you're going to love it."

"I cannot believe he told you. No fair keeping secrets."

"Not secrets. Surprises."

"I hate surprises."

"You love surprises. If I told you, you'd be completely bummed out because I ruined the surprise, and you know it."

She twisted her lips into a pout and folded her arms, giving him her best bratty attitude. Finally she rolled her eyes, because he kinda had a point.

"Yeah, okay." She checked the time on her cellphone. "We should get going. They're probably already in the restaurant."

Simon grabbed his room key.

"I'm ready. You know, I'm surprised you stopped by my room first, instead of going to Aunt Bobbie's room."

"Well, I was excited to see you too, big brother. I wanted a few minutes alone with you first."

"Aww!"

Simon made a moony face at her and wrapped his arm around her shoulders, pulling her in for a hug that morphed into a noogie.

Sidney wrestled out of his hold, slapping at his arms.

"Never mind! I take it back, you big weenie."

Simon cracked up laughing.

She rushed to the mirror to fix her mass of curls.

"No take backs. You said you love me. Can't take it back. Not how it works."

Simon's tone was all business as he spouted off the no-take-backs rule that had governed their childhoods.

"Those love words never came out of my mouth!"

"Didn't have to. It was implied."

He opened the door for her, and Sidney whacked him in the arm again as they stepped out into the hallway and headed for the elevator.

Down in the opulent lobby they made their way to the hotel's five-star restaurant and back to the private dining room. Sidney squeezed Simon's hand and took a deep breath before she stepped inside.

Her Aunt and Uncle and two cousins were inspecting the overflowing buffet spread that a restaurant server was putting the final touches on, and didn't see them enter.

"Good morning, family."

They all turned at once.

Screeches and whoops of joy pierced the air, and they descended on Sidney and Simon like a swarm of birds.

Hugs, kisses, laughter, tears, and everyone talking at once.

"Look at you!"

"...just as handsome as ever!"

"Y'all a sight for sore eyes!"

"...so good to see you!"

"You went natural!"

"Girl, your curls are slammin'!"

"...gotten so big!"

"My sister would be so happy today!"

It was small, controlled chaos, and Sidney's heart felt like a sponge, happily soaking up every last drop of it. Oh, how she had missed these people.

By the time they settled down, there wasn't a dry eye in the room, and Sidney even caught the restaurant server shoot them all a heartwarming smile as she quietly exited the room.

"Oh, Sidney," her Aunt Bobbie dabbed at a few tears with a tissue. "You look so good, honey."

"Thank you."

"And just look at my handsome nephew!" Bobbie placed a hand on Simon's cheek. "*Major* Simon Fairchild. Oh, Dawn would be so proud of you both."

"It's good to see you, Auntie." Simon kissed the woman's cheek and then turned to her husband and smiled. "Uncle Frank. What's going on, man?"

Sidney smiled at the reunion and wiped her own tears. Then Tameka touched her arm.

"Sid. Simon. This is my husband, Jamal. I know you met him a long time ago, Sid, but I thought reintroductions were in order."

They both shook hands with the dark-skinned man Tameka was obviously crazy about.

"Good to meet you," Jamal said, shaking Simon's hand. Then

he turned to Sidney. "And good to re-meet you! Also best wishes to you."

"Thank you so much! Since we all reconnected on the phone a couple of months ago, this one talks about you and Jabari all the time." She gestured to Tameka. "You obviously make her very happy."

"I do my best." Jamal wrapped his arm around Tameka.

Sidney bent down and smiled at the four-year-old little boy watching everything so intently.

"Hi Jabari. I'm Sidney. I'm your mommy's cousin."

"I know."

"The last time I saw you, you were a tiny baby, and I could practically hold you in one hand."

The boy looked at her like he didn't believe he'd ever been so small.

"I want to thank you for agreeing to be in my wedding."

A big smile broke out on his face and then he hid behind his mother's leg.

"Sidney, when do we get to meet his man of yours?" Erika asked.

"Okay, so, Isaac is working today. He does plan to swing by soon to meet everybody, but we have no idea how long he'll be able to stay. It just depends on if he gets a call. But he will be here."

Everyone seemed pleased to know they'd get to meet her intended, but Sidney knew she needed to say more.

"Oh, and please remember what I told you all about the touching thing, okay? I know it sounds weird to you, but it's very important to him. Therefore it is very important to me. No hand-shakes, no hugs. Not unless Ike initiates it himself, okay?"

"We remember," Bobbie said, nodding to affirm her statement.

"Sid, this hotel is top of the line," Tameka said, changing the subject. "I'm impressed."

Sidney grinned, remembering that Tameka always did have

expensive tastes, as evidenced by her stylish, designer outfit, perfect nails and make-up. She could've just stepped off a high-fashion runway.

"Good. I'm glad you're happy with it."

"Very. And this brunch spread looks delicious, girl. I'm about to dive in because I am starving."

"Yes, please! Everyone, let's eat up."

She gestured to the buffet to get them moving that way.

"Help yourselves. I ordered a little bit of everything so that we'd have a variety to choose from. There should be something for everybody's tastes."

The buffet was sumptuous with light and fluffy scrambled eggs, bacon, sausage, and ham, Belgium waffles, french toast, and eggs Benedict. There was even a do-it-yourself omelet station, coffee, juice, and champagne mimosas.

"Oh, Sidney, you're not paying for this brunch yourself, are you? This couldn't have been cheap." Plate in hand, Aunt Bobbie looked concerned.

"Actually, my favorite brother is footing the bill for our family brunch reunion today."

Sidney smiled up at Simon.

"Oh, okay, Major. I see you."

Bobbie's tone was clearly impressed, and Simon smiled.

"Yeah, Simon, why don't you let us reimburse you for this, man?" Uncle Frank said.

"No." Simon shook his head.

"Yes. We can at least go in half with you, honey," Aunt Bobbie insisted.

"No!" Simon's voice was forceful as he loaded up his plate. "You will do no such thing. This is part of my wedding gift to Sid. So, don't even trip."

Sidney leaned over and planted a kiss on Simon's cheek.

Once they all had full plates they found seats around the long dining table, and a happy chatter rose around them as they ate and laughed and talked and got caught up on each other's lives.

They were in the middle of discussing the week-long wedding festivities when a man suddenly walked into their midst and loomed nearby.

Sidney looked up at him and her smile froze.

This couldn't be right.

Who?

How?

Was this for real?

Anger clawed at the joy in her heart.

The man was mid-to-late sixties. Lighter in skin tone than her or Simon — the shade some black folks would often call 'high yella'. Short, soft curly hair. Light brown, champagne-colored eyes. Handsome.

His awkward smile came easy, the kind usually held by men who believed their charm was their superpower. His manner of dress was what Sidney would call dressy casual. Almost as if he'd been invited to a special gathering.

"Hey. Is this a private family breakfast or is there room for me?"

Simon was on his feet before Sidney could stop him.

"What the hell are you doing here?"

He didn't raise his voice, but the words were vicious.

The man stepped further in. "Well, I heard my little girl was getting married, and I thought maybe my invitation got lost in the mail."

He looked at Sidney and smiled, and her stomach pitched dangerously.

"Hi, babygirl."

"Don't you babygirl her." Simon's voice rose a couple of octaves, clearly pissed. "Get the hell out of here!"

Sidney got to her feet, taking Simon by the arm to try and calm him down. She turned and glared at the intruder.

"Carlton, right?"

He seemed momentarily stunned, and then nodded.

"That's right."

Sidney's stomach lurched again.

It was true.

He was really here.

"What are you doing here?" she asked him.

"Like I said…"

"Simon and I haven't seen you since we were kids. Why would you expect to be invited to my wedding? For that matter, how do you think I would even know where to send an invitation? How the hell do you even know that I'm getting married? Or even what hotel to find us in, let alone what city?"

Carlton's gaze flitted briefly over to Bobbie.

The sheepish, guilty expression on Bobbie's face told Sidney all she needed to know. She had to take a deep breath to keep from losing her breakfast.

"You invited him to my wedding without asking me?"

"No!"

"And you invited him here to brunch with the family? How could you do this to me?"

"Sidney, I didn't."

"Did it occur to you that Simon and I might not be happy about this? What the hell were you thinking, Aunty Bobbie?"

She was practically yelling now, but she couldn't help it.

Bobbie got to her feet and reached out her hands, palm out, to calm her.

"No. No, I did not invite him! I ran into Carlton about a week ago at a store in LA, and I guess I mentioned that we were all coming to Cleveland for your wedding. But that is all I said! I did not imply that he should come too. And I certainly did not invite him here to brunch!"

Bobbie looked over at Carlton with a hateful glare.

"After the way he walked out on my sister and you kids, I

would never blindside you like that, Sidney. You know me better than that, honey." Bobbie looked at Carlton again. "How did you know to come here? What? Did you follow us?"

Carlton gestured toward her.

"You may not remember our entire conversation, Bobbie, but you did mention to me that you would all be having brunch this morning after your flight got in. I called a lot of hotels when I got here last night, looking for the one hosting a family breakfast in a private room this morning."

"You son of a bitch."

Simon moved to walk around the table, but Sidney stood in his way, pushing on his chest while Uncle Frank held him back.

"You think you just gonna roll up in here and crash our family gathering, and we're gonna let you insert yourself in the middle of things?"

"Look, Simon, I know you're pissed at me, but..."

"Pissed?" Simon cut him off. "Motherfucker, we ain't seen you since we was knee-high. Don't nobody care enough about you to be pissed! We just don't want you here. Now get the fuck out before I come over there and throw you out!"

The struggle to contain him was getting harder, and Sidney knew she had to say or do something.

"Simon! Stop it. Calm down."

His gaze snapped to hers.

"What?" He looked like she'd spit in his face. "You want him here?"

"No, I don't. But more than that? I don't want you tossed in jail for assault the week of my wedding, okay? Please calm down."

She stared into his eyes and silently willed him to listen to reason.

"Sidney? Everything okay in here?"

The sound of Isaac's voice made everything better.

She whirled around to see him standing behind Carlton in the doorway.

"Isaac."

She left Simon and rushed into his arms.

"I am so glad you're here."

Isaac kissed her lips, but Sidney noticed his eyes were still focused on the heated crowd. Ever the cop.

"Tempers seem sort of high, darlin'. What's going on?"

She took him by the hand and led him further into the room. Stepping past Carlton, she walked over to her family and wrapped her arm around Isaac's waist.

"Everyone, this is my Isaac."

She smiled up at him, but she felt the nerves and anxiety of the last few moments threatening to drown her, and she knew that Ike could feel it too with that overdeveloped sense of empathy of his.

He smiled at everyone and offered his hand to none of them.

"Ike, this is Aunt Bobbie and Uncle Frank Minter. My cousin Erika Minter. And my cousin Tameka and her husband, Jamal Turner. And the handsome little one is Jabari."

She looked up at Ike again and smiled.

"And they've all been briefed on your aversion to shaking hands, so there's no pressure."

Ike kissed her forehead and greeted her family with a smile and a wave.

"It's nice to finally meet everyone. Sid's been telling me all about y'all."

They all greeted him warmly, but Sidney was certain that he could still feel the tension sitting on top of the room.

"Wait, hold up." Carlton spoke as if on cue. "You're marrying a white guy?"

Sidney turned around and glared at him, but Simon spoke up before she could even form words.

"You got a problem with that? Like it's any of your business."

Carlton raised his hands in surrender and looked at Simon.

"I just didn't know. I'm surprised, that's all." He turned back to Sidney and Isaac. "I apologize."

Sidney felt Isaac's body tense slightly and he stared Carlton in the eyes.

"Sid?"

"Isaac, this is Carlton Fairchild. A surprise guest, and... my father."

That had his attention zipping right to her, and she could see the mild shock in his gorgeous grey eyes.

"Your *father?*"

Sidney understood his confusion. She'd told him all about how her father had never been in the picture.

"Surprise."

There was no laughter or joy in her tone, and she didn't care.

Carlton stuck out his hand and smiled.

Isaac ignored the gesture and stared at him.

"Ike doesn't like to shake hands," Sidney said flatly.

Carlton frowned at him. "Why the hell not?"

"Because he doesn't," Sidney snapped. "And you never answered my question, Carlton. What are you doing here?"

Carlton sighed and looked down for a second, and Sidney saw a flash of something in his eyes. Something she couldn't name.

"When I heard you were getting married, I just wanted to see you. Both of you." He glanced over at Simon before looking at Sidney again. "I know it's been a long time, and that's on me. But weddings are nice family occasions, and I just wanted to come walk my babygirl down the aisle, that's all."

He smiled at her and held his arms wide, as if waiting for a hug.

"Well then you came a long way for nothing," Simon spoke up. "*I'm* walking Sidney down the aisle. As it should be."

Carlton turned on him.

"No, it *should* be her father. Every little girl wants that."

He turned back to Sidney, who stood frozen and horrified.

Was he for real?

"And since I missed the opportunity to do it the first time you got married, I thought this would be perfect. Come on, now, every father wants to do this for his little girl."

"Yeah, every *father* does," Simon countered. "But you were never a father to her! You couldn't be bothered by a wife and two kids. You didn't want to be tied down, remember? You had too many other women to chase. Too many bigger and better things to pursue."

Things went down hill from there.

The yelling match escalated quickly, with Uncle Frank and Jamal struggling to hold Simon back as he threatened to climb over the table to get his hands around Carlton's throat.

Sidney clutched her temples, tears springing to her eyes.

Erika wrapped her arms around Sidney's shoulders.

"All right, that's enough!"

Isaac stepped forward, cop voice fully engaged, and snagged everyone's attention.

He looked at Simon.

"Simon! Don't make me break up this party in an official capacity. Come on, man. I don't want to cuff you."

His southern twang deepened, and he stared his future brother-in-law down.

Simon glared at him for a long moment, then backed away from the table.

"And you."

Isaac pointed at Carlton.

"I'd like to throw you out for disrupting this reunion and upsetting Sidney. But I'll take my cues from her instead."

He kept his eyes on Carlton and addressed Sidney.

"What do you want to happen here, darlin'?"

Sidney wrapped her arms around herself and tried not to feel like everything had been ruined. She understood Simon's stance on things, but part of her was more inclined to hear Carlton out than throw him out.

She wiped a hand over her cheek and sniffed. Isaac took the dark blue bandana-style handkerchief from his pocket and handed it to her. Gratefully, she took it and wiped her nose.

"He can stay." Her voice was small and full of trepidation.

"What the fuck...?"

Simon sounded pissed, but Isaac snapped and pointed a finger at him, shutting him up once again.

Carlton's big, relieved smile had Sidney pointing her own finger at her father.

"Not so fast. I will allow you to come to my wedding, if that's what you choose. But Simon will be walking me down the aisle. Is that clear?"

Carlton looked deflated. "But, Sidney..."

"Is. That. Clear?"

"Yes. Of course." Carlton finally backed down. "Thank you, for letting me stay."

"Don't make me regret it."

Sidney took Isaac's hand and led him to a corner of the room to steal a few moments of calm.

Isaac gently took her face in both his hands and looked into her eyes.

"You okay?"

Still sniffing, Sidney sighed and rolled her eyes. She could feel more tears swimming in them, but she didn't want to cry anymore.

"I'm fine."

"No, you're not. And I can't blame you. That was a hell of a thing to walk in on."

"I can imagine."

"Interesting way to meet my new in-laws. Especially since I was not expecting to meet your..."

"Sperm donor?" Sidney interrupted him. "Yeah, me either."

Isaac caressed her face and kissed her lips.

"I'm sorry, baby."

"Hey. None of this is your fault, darlin'. Not one part."

"I know. I just can't believe he had the balls to show up here. You know, I was probably five years old the last time I saw that man?"

"Really?"

"Well... no. I did see him once when I was about thirteen. Simon and I were hanging out on the stoop of our apartment building with our friends, and he was there across the square with this group of men. They were shooting craps." She paused and shook her head, fighting back more tears. "I didn't even know who he was until Simon pointed him out to me. How fucked up is that?"

"Did he see you?"

"From the way he stopped and stared at us, I knew that he must've known exactly who we were. But he never made a move to come speak to us. So neither did we."

She paused and glanced over at Carlton.

"And today he just shows up and expects to walk me down the aisle like we're family? Who does that?"

Isaac pulled her closer, drawing her attention, and rested his forehead against hers.

"Hey. You just say the word and he's out of here. You want him locked up for the week until we're off on our honeymoon? I can probably make that happen."

Sidney giggled in spite of her jumbled emotions about her father, and looked up into Isaac's eyes.

"Thanks for the offer, but I don't think it'll be necessary."

"You sure? I got no problem finding some trumped up charges to arrest him on."

"I'd rather not have my groom arrested for falsifying evidence, if you don't mind."

Ike shrugged a shoulder.

"Okay. The offer stands though."

She giggled again.

"I'll keep it in mind. Thanks for making me laugh."

"Anything for you."

He ran his fingertips over her cheek.

"Come on. Let's get you a plate and sit down."

"Okay."

They hit the buffet, and then took a seat at the table, where Carlton had also helped himself to the food.

As they ate, Sidney noticed Simon and Carlton eyeing each other — one with contempt, the other with what she would maybe describe as... regret? Was it possible that Carlton regretted walking out on them?

The truce was holding at any rate, tension still hovering over them amid the now stiff small talk.

"So, Isaac," Frank smiled at him. "Simon was telling me about the tour of the sports stadiums that your father set up for us guys while the ladies are doing wedding things later today."

"Oh, yeah. It's a good tour, I've been on it. You guys will have fun."

"I'm sorry you won't be joining us. Sidney says you're on duty today."

"Yeah, I could only get two weeks off, so we decided to use them both for the honeymoon."

"Makes sense to me, Ike," Erika spoke up.

"Say, Ike, are you born and raised here in Cleveland?" Frank asked.

"Oh, no, sir. My family is originally from Tennessee. We relocated here when I was about ten."

"So, that explains that little twang I hear," Frank laughed.

Isaac grinned at him. "Yes, sir."

"And Sidney tells us you're a decorated police detective." Bobbie sounded impressed again. "You enjoy that line of work?"

Before Isaac could form a response, Carlton interjected.

"Oh, you gotta be shitting me. A white *cop?*" He looked over at Sidney, putting his fork down with a clank. "That's who you're marrying?"

Sidney glared at him wishing her looks could kill.

"If you're not happy with my choice, please by all means, leave."

Carlton ignored the warning in her voice and looked at Isaac.

"I'm sorry. This is nothing against you personally. I'm sure you're a decent guy."

He turned back to Sidney.

"But you know what they're doing to us out there, right? You watch the news? You see all the black and brown brothas out there getting shot down by white cops all over the country?"

He turned his heated gaze on Simon and Frank, since Sidney clearly wasn't listening.

"Does anybody at this table know what I'm talking about?"

Sidney had had enough.

"We all know what you're talking about, Carlton. But see, the thing is... it's got no bearing on who I love or who I choose to marry. Much like how your opinion has no bearing on who I am, or how I choose to live my life."

She pointed a finger at him and looked him in the eyes.

"That's the second racist outburst you've made here today, and it's not acceptable. One more and you're done. I will not have you here all week souring my wedding and insulting my fiancé and his family. Do you understand me?"

Carlton opened his mouth to say something, but he must've thought better of it because he closed his mouth and took a breath. He licked his lips and looked down at his plate.

"Sidney asked you a question." Simon stared at him.

Carlton met Simon's gaze and then turned to Sidney.

"I understand."

"I think you owe Isaac an apology," Sidney said.

Carlton nodded and looked at Isaac.

"I do apologize, Isaac. I'm sure you've never even shot a black man."

Isaac cocked an eyebrow as he stared at his future father-in-law.

"Well, not one that didn't deserve it."

Carlton frowned. "Was that a joke?"

"Was your apology a joke? Because it felt more like a dig."

They glared at each other for a long moment, and Sidney held her breath. Finally Isaac's cellphone rang. He pulled it from a pocket and answered, still staring at Carlton in a peculiar way.

"Taylor."

Sidney placed her hand on Ike's leg and listened to his side of the brief conversation. Something about a strip mall. He ended the call and looked at Sidney.

"I'm afraid I've got to go. Shooting at a strip mall."

He picked up a piece of bacon from his plate and kissed Sidney's lips.

"You remember my offer, okay? It still stands. Now more than ever."

Sidney smiled at him. "I will."

"I love you."

"I love you back."

He kissed her again and stood, glancing around the table.

"My apologies, but I have to go back to work. It was nice meeting everyone. Almost."

The dig was so subtle, Sidney wasn't even sure anyone else caught it, but it made her smile.

"I look forward to seeing you all again this week during the festivities." Isaac motioned to Simon before taking a bite of bacon. "Simon... call me later, man."

Simon nodded.

"And um..." Isaac nodded in Sidney's direction.

Sidney understood his silent gesture, and she could see that Simon did too.

"Oh, don't worry. I got her."

Satisfied with that response, Isaac winked at her and left.

When he was gone, Carlton muttered, "A white cop. I did not expect that."

Sidney flopped back in her chair.

"I didn't expect you either, but here you are."

9

*I*saac left the hotel and headed for his car, wondering what the odds were that the cops would be called to break up the fight at Sidney's reunion brunch. She had been looking forward to that gathering with the eager anticipation of a kid at Christmastime. He hated that her long lost father had chosen to invite himself and ruin it for her.

And what the heck was with that guy anyway? Just the thought of him had Isaac's blood boiling. The man was downright rude.

And racist.

But there was something else there too. Something Isaac intrinsically felt when he looked at the man. He was broken somehow.

It was the only way he could think to describe what he felt, and he knew it didn't make any sense. But that man was broken, and desperate, and sad. And knowing that, made him worry for Sidney.

Pulling up at the strip mall, he pushed it aside and centered his thoughts on his job. Another shooting in broad daylight. And what were the odds this one was related to the two from yesterday? For his money, it was a sure thing.

He crossed the police tape and walked over to where Pete was already talking to a uniformed officer.

"What we got, Pete?"

"Two dead, five others wounded, one seriously." Pete pointed to the paramedics rushing a stretcher into a waiting EMT bus. "Same story as yesterday. Witnesses describe gun, but not the shooter. I've already pulled IDs from our victims."

He handed Isaac two IDs in sealed evidence bags.

Isaac studied the IDs for a moment, noting that one of the victims was a young woman.

"This game is getting old real fast. It's almost starting to feel like we're being toyed with. Something's not right here."

He glanced around the scene. A large section of the parking lot had been roped off with police tape, and there were two bodies on the ground being gone over by CSU. Multiple wounded being tended to by EMTs. Isaac shook his head and took it all in.

"Something's not right."

He looked over at his partner.

"Let's head back to the station. While you run our vics, I'm going to get on the wire and maybe comb through some old cases. See what pops out at me."

Pete stared at him, face like stone, and gave an almost undetectable nod.

They headed to their respective cars, and Isaac glanced over at Pete once more.

"You okay?"

"What?"

"You seem a little distracted today."

"Is that not allowed?"

Isaac raised an eyebrow on another sideways glance. Pete's irritated tone said he was itching for a fight, but Ike had no intention of sparring.

"You're allowed."

"Thanks for your permission."

Pete jerked open the driver's door of his car and slammed it once he was in. Then he took off without any preamble.

Isaac stared after him wondering what the heck that was all about. He got into his own car and headed to the station.

By the time Isaac got to the detectives pit, Pete was already at his desk, stabbing the keys of his computer like he was using a knife. Isaac sighed and sat down and turned to his own computer.

He searched the PD's database for similar crimes, but nothing of any note came up. Out of curiosity, he expanded his search to NCIC — the National Crime Information Center. It took nearly half an hour, but he finally found some info on a ten-victim shooting spree from 20 years ago in Philadelphia.

In that spree, the shooter confessed and described the gun in reverent terms. But what caught Isaac's eye was that the description of the gun was the exact same description of the gun they'd been getting from all witnesses in this case. The shooter in the Philadelphia case also told the cops where he'd ditched the gun. An extensive search ensued, but the gun was never recovered.

Interestingly, 18 years before the Philadelphia case, there was a similar case reported in Bangor, Maine.

Isaac glanced up to tell Pete what he'd stumbled on, but one look at the scowl on his partner's face had him zipping his lips tight.

He needed a sounding board, and Pete was in no mood. With a sigh, he stood and left the pit. He headed down one floor to the SWAT commander's office and knocked on the open door.

Franklin Ross looked up from behind his desk and stared at him.

Isaac had no beef with Ross. Although standing in the man's doorway, he was reminded of an incident from a couple of months ago when Sidney and Bree were being held hostage at Hope House by a crazed abusive husband. He and Ross had butted heads that day over the fact that Isaac refused to back down and let SWAT do its job. Instead, he'd talked his way inside the house, delivered Bree's baby, and took out the suspect with his budding telekinesis.

Ross hadn't been too happy with him, but he'd gotten the job done. He'd do it all again if it meant keeping Sidney safe.

"What can I do for you, Taylor?"

Isaac stepped into the office and clasped his hands in front of him.

"Sorry to bother you, but I seem to remember hearing that you are something of a gun historian. Is that right?"

Ross squinted at him, suspicious, but clearly intrigued.

"What of it?"

"Well, I've got myself a mystery of sorts, and I was hoping you could help me out."

"With?"

Isaac took a breath and launched into the details of the shooting spree.

"And the kicker is that not a single witness can describe the shooter, but they all describe the gun in great detail."

Ross raised a hand to stop him.

"Wait. Is this gun a Colt .45?"

Isaac cocked his head.

"Okay, I thought I was supposed to be the freaky psychic one."

To his shock, Ross nearly busted a gut laughing. Amused, Isaac just stood watching the man crack up.

"I didn't think you could make fun of yourself, Taylor!" Ross belted out once he'd composed himself. "I thought you were a conceited hard ass."

"Funny. I was just thinking how shocked I am to see that you know how to laugh."

Ross grinned at him and gestured to the chair in front of his desk.

"Sit down, Taylor. You ever hear of the Cursed Colt?"

Isaac took a seat with a frown.

"The what?"

"There are rumors in the gun world about a gun known as the Cursed Colt. It's a very ornate, gold-plated Colt .45 with ivory grips. And it's cursed."

"The gun itself is cursed?"

"That's the rumor. Supposedly, it was presented to Al Capone as a gift in 1926. No one's sure who gave it to him or exactly when it left his possession, but the gun turns up in a random city around the country every 20 years or so. Always as the subject of a brief and bloody murder spree."

Ross paused, and Isaac just stared at him.

Was this a joke?

"The shooter is eventually caught," Ross continued, "but the gun is never recovered. As the story goes, the gun is said to be so beautiful that it hypnotizes whoever handles it and compels them to commit murder."

Isaac couldn't stand it anymore.

"That's bullshit."

Ross shrugged a shoulder and grinned.

"Sounds like bullshit to you and me. But how many dead bodies you got?"

Isaac sighed and tallied up the body count.

"Seven dead, nine wounded, one likely."

"And no suspects yet?"

"Ross, are you telling me you honestly believe this Cursed Colt actually exists?"

"I'm just relaying information. I've actually got a file on it somewhere. Hang on."

He got up and flipped through a file cabinet, pulling out a fairly thick file.

"Yeah, here it is." He handed the file to Isaac. "Just some personal research I did on the subject a few years back. There's documentation in there on sightings of the Colt from several cities going back to 1942. All unexplained shooting sprees where the weapon — the afore mentioned Colt — is never found."

Isaac flipped through the file with more than a passing curiosity.

Curses.

First, a supposed family curse going back nearly a hundred years, and now a cursed gun compelling people to murder.

"There's just one problem with this theory, Ross."

"What's that?"

"Curses aren't real." Isaac closed the file and looked Ross in the eyes. "I can't build motive on a curse."

"I don't know what to tell you, Sergeant. You came in here with a question and I answered it to the best of my ability."

Isaac sighed and stood.

"Well, thanks. Mind if I hang onto this for a while?"

"Just remember where it lives."

"You'll get it back."

Isaac took the file and left Ross' office. He took the stairs back up to the fourth floor just in time to see Pete punch the vending machine like a prizefighter.

"Whoa! Hey, what is wrong with you today, man?"

Pete whirled around and glared at him.

"Nothing's wrong!" He kicked the machine once more for good measure.

"Right."

Pete huffed out a breath.

"Everything's wrong."

"Did you and Jada have a fight or something?"

"What? No. I'd be fine if this thing would just give me the damn candy bar I just paid for!"

He hauled off and punched it again.

Isaac glanced at the stuck candy bar wedged on the coil. He fished fifty cents from his pocket and fed it into the machine. The candy bar dropped, along with the one behind it. Isaac tucked the file under his arm and stooped to grab the candy. Gingerly, he held both bars out to his partner.

"There, now you got two of them."

Pete snatched the candy, causing Ike to jerk his hand back to avoid the touch.

"Thanks."

"Yep. You want to talk about whatever's eating at you?"

Pete sighed and leaned back against the wall, and Isaac noted that he looked very much like a scared, angry little boy in that moment.

"It's my moms." Pete's voice was quiet now. All the fight gone. "The cancer is back. Doctor's tossing out words like 'stage three,' whatever the hell that means."

"Oh, Pete. I'm sorry to hear that. Julieta's a sweet lady. Sid and I like her a lot."

Pete nodded. "She likes you and Sid too. She bought a new dress for your wedding. She's excited Sid invited her."

Isaac smiled, but he could see the worry and the fear all over Pete. It was etched in his face and dragging down his body.

"Listen, Pete... Julieta strikes me as a very strong woman. Determined and purposeful, both in her words and in her actions. She's a fighter."

Pete finally looked him in the eyes.

"Thanks for saying that. I apologize for the attitude. Guess I'm just angry at the whole damn world today."

"No apologies necessary."

They moved back through the pit to their desks, and Pete ripped open a candy bar.

"Where'd you go anyway?"

"I went down to talk to Franklin Ross about the gun in our shooting spree case."

"Oh, yeah?"

"You are not going to believe what he told me."

When they sat down, he handed the file to Pete and told him all that Ross had said. Pete flipped through it and glanced up at him.

"So you don't believe any of this curse crap, right?"

Isaac looked at him. "Do you?"

Pete polished off one candy bar and sighed.

"I don't know, man. I mean... I didn't really believe in psychics until I met you."

Pete's words felt like the sharp sting of a hornet — pinching and growing more painful by the second.

It was an inconvenient truth Isaac couldn't escape.

"Yeah. Neither did I."

He sat back in his seat and thought about that. He had no clue how to reconcile any of it.

"But curses? I mean, what the heck are we supposed to do here? Take this file on a supposedly cursed Colt .45 into Hayes' office and tell him we found our killer? The gun made him do it? And while we're at it, let's just close up the Townsend-witch's-curse case too."

Isaac snatched the second candy bar from Pete's desk, flopped back in his chair and tore into it.

"I know you're frustrated, Ike. But the gun described in the police reports and news clippings in this file sound an awful lot like the description of the gun we keep coming up against in this case."

"Yeah, well, be that as it may... I refuse to believe we're dealing with a curse. On either one of these cases."

"Well, in *this* case, in all those reports, the shooter eventually confesses. Maybe all we have to do is sit back and wait for it."

Isaac rolled his eyes.

"Yeah. Let's do that."

———

It had been almost two months since Detective Gerri Miller had been cleared by the department shrink and allowed to begin her new position with the Special Victims Unit of the Violent Crimes Division. So far, things were going great. The work really wasn't that much different from what she'd been doing before in Homicide, and it was great being able to still see her buddies from her old unit — and Gavin — every day in the detectives pit.

Not that everything was a breeze.

It was weird getting used to a new partner and a new lieutenant. It was especially weird stepping into the detectives pit every day and not seeing Curt Dorn's cocky smile at the desk next to hers.

She truly missed her former partner, but she supposed that would always be true. She knew she would never forget him. Not his man-sized ego or his infectious laugh. Not the things he'd taught her about being a good detective. And certainly not the way he'd died in her arms, shot down by a misguided fellow cop.

She shrugged the sorrow off her shoulders and followed her new partner, Tina Mayfield, through the pit and into her new lieutenant's office.

They'd just come from seeing a victim through the perils of a line up. For weeks, the teenaged girl had been incredibly reluctant to speak with them at all, let alone identify her rapist. And her mother had been like a mama lion, wanting to spare the girl any further pain. But Gerri had personally spent a great deal of time talking to each of them, trying to convince the young girl to stand up and put the man away so that he couldn't hurt anyone else.

"Excellent work on this, Miller."

Lieutenant Jo Haftel stood from behind her desk and looked Gerri in the eyes. She had the build and stature of an athlete, Gerri decided. And her shoulder-length auburn hair was buzzed on one side. A style not many could convincingly pull off, yet it worked on Haftel.

"Truly. I didn't think we'd ever get the victim to speak up on this one and finger her rapist, but... somehow you got her to open up. I know there are two girls willing to talk, but the DA says Grace's testimony alone will put this guy away for a long, long time."

Gerri took in a deep breath, trying to tamp down the swell of pride in her chest. It wasn't the first time she'd been praised for a job well done, but it was more rewarding somehow after all she'd been through with Curt's death.

"And you," Haftel continued, "are quickly proving yourself to be an asset to our Special Victims team. Well done."

"Thank you, Lieutenant. I really appreciate you taking a chance on me for this position."

"An experienced homicide detective like yourself? It was a no-brainer on my part. Keep up the good work."

"Yes, ma'am."

"After shift, you two should go have a beer. You earned it."

She smiled at them, and Gerri followed her new partner out into the pit once again.

At their desks, Tina Mayfield turned around and smiled at her.

Tina was tall and stocky, the type of woman you wouldn't want to piss off if she was having a bad day. Her skin had a slight olive tone to it, but Gerri couldn't say for sure what her ethnic make-up might be. Her hair was the color of red bricks, and when it wasn't pulled back into a severe French braid, Gerri would wager that it was wavy or frizzy in texture. She had brown eyes, and a small spattering of freckles on her nose. Her face was interesting, and Gerri decided she liked her.

"Good work, partner."

Gerri smiled. "You were there too. Pat yourself on the back. Mayfield and Miller might make a great detective team, yeah?"

"You don't have to do that. We both know this win was all you. And I think that's great."

Tina gave her a genuine smile, and Gerri swallowed down the awkwardness and nodded in appreciation.

"Well, thanks."

"You know, I read your file when I found out you were going to be my new partner."

"Yeah? I read yours too. Impressive."

"Right back at ya. You had a solid record in homicide, so I'm sure you'll continue to do great here in Special Victims."

"So far, I'm really enjoying the work. I'm actually finding it even more rewarding than homicide somehow. I think it'll be a great fit."

"That's good." Tina smiled at her. Then that same smile turned treacherous. "Yeah, it's too bad Haftel's a woman, though, huh? You won't be able to sleep your way up the ranks here."

Gerri's stomach caved in like she'd been sucker punched.

Tina turned and walked away.

Gerri stared after her wondering what the fuck had just happened?

10

Sidney drove to the bridal shop, relieved and happy to leave the disastrous reunion brunch behind her.

Except that it wasn't behind her.

Not with Aunt Bobbie, Erika, and Tameka along for the ride.

She couldn't exactly escape them. Not once they found out that her next stop was the bridal shop to pick up her wedding dress. They wanted to tag along and have her put it on so that they could see it before the wedding.

And honestly, at any other time, Sidney would've been excited to bring them along and model the gown for them. She *was* excited. But she also couldn't let go of the knowledge that Carlton Fairchild had shown up uninvited, crashed their brunch reunion, angered Simon, and insulted Isaac, all because Aunt Bobbie had shot her mouth off when she ran into him at a grocery store.

She sighed and drove on.

Bobbie hadn't done it on purpose. She knew that. And she was trying very hard not to have an attitude with the woman who'd been her surrogate mom for several years after her real mother had been killed by a drunk driver.

She loved her Aunt Bobbie. More importantly, she knew that Bobbie loved her as much as her own daughters.

"This is silly," she mumbled.

"What? What's silly, honey?"

Sidney glanced over at Bobbie in the passenger seat.

"Huh? Did I say something out loud? I'm sorry."

Bobbie smiled at her. "Oh, Sidney, you're not still talking to yourself, are you?"

Sidney grinned. "I don't do it as much as I used to. But it slips out occasionally." She shrugged her shoulders. "Habit."

Bobbie laughed at her, and Sidney's anxiety over the disastrous brunch began to ebb away.

"There's the bridal shop."

Stopped at a red light, she pointed to a shop on the corner up ahead.

"I bet Bree's already there."

"Now, who is Bree?"

"Oh, Bree is my very good friend and future sister-in-law. She's married to Ike's brother, Adam. She's my matron of honor."

Her stomach fluttered with hope at the thought that she'd be picking up her wedding dress in just a few more minutes.

For her wedding.

Her wedding that was happening in four days.

The flutters turned to ripples.

Ripples to waves.

"Oh, I can't wait for you to see my wedding gown!"

Her sing-songy voice was full of happy excitement.

"This shop is owned by a designer who only makes one of a kind dresses, so that every bride is unique. My dress is gorgeous!"

"Oh, it sounds marvelous," Bobbie said.

Tameka spoke up from the backseat. "Hey, Sid, where was Simon taking Dad, Jamal and Jabari again?"

"They're going on some kind of tour of all the sports stadiums in Cleveland, since the city has three professional teams. It's something Ike's dad offered to do for Simon a few weeks ago. Apparently they get to see the stadiums and visit the gift shops. They might even get to see an athlete or two if Ike's dad could arrange it."

"Ike's dad got it like that?"

"Well, he works with the Cleveland Indians organization."

"Oh, okay. I don't know nothing about football."

Sidney giggled. "That's baseball."

Laughter filled the car and Sidney pulled into the dress shop parking lot. Before she could get her seatbelt off, Bobbie reached over and took her arm.

"Sidney? I really am sorry about Carlton crashing our brunch. If I'd had any idea that he would do something so foolish I never would've mentioned a word to him about your wedding."

Sidney wanted to let it go, but she just couldn't. She turned in her seat to look her aunt in the eyes.

"Why did you though? I mean, why did you feel the need to say anything at all?"

"I don't know." Bobbie shook her head, and her voice held so much remorse. "I've just been so happy lately since you got back in touch with us again. I've been thinking a lot about Dawn."

Sidney could understand that, at least. Her mom was always close to her own thoughts, and she had been more so since the wedding planning began.

"I think about how she raised you and Simon all on her own after Carlton walked out on her."

"He walked out on all of us, Aunt Bobbie."

"I know. I guess when I ran into him that day, I just wanted to rub his face in it. In what all he was missing out on by choosing not to be a father to you and Simon. I wanted him to be jealous that he wasn't included. It was selfish, and I'm sorry."

Sidney sighed and took her hand.

"It's okay, Auntie. Truly. We're okay."

They shared a hug, and Sidney finally felt the anger evaporate. She couldn't stay mad at the only mother figure she had left.

"Let's go. We've got a wedding dress to fawn over."

Just outside the door of the bridal shop, Bree Taylor waited with baby Isla in one of those one-shouldered fabric carriers that cradled the baby against her.

"Hey! There you are."

Her bright smile had Sidney instantly in a better mood, and she hugged her, being careful not to crush Isla.

"Bree, I'd like you to meet my Aunt Bobbie, and my cousins Erika and Tameka. Everyone, this is Bree Taylor, my future sister-in-law and matron of honor."

There were handshakes and greetings all around. Bobbie took Isla's tiny hand.

"And who is this?"

"This is Isla." Bree beamed and the baby cooed. "She's two and a half months old and super excited to be in on all this wedding hoopla."

"Then let's do it!" Sidney said.

Laughter and happy chatter followed them into the shop, and Sidney headed straight for the counter and smiled at the woman standing there.

"Hi. I'm Sidney Fairchild. I'm here to pick up my wedding gown, but I was wondering if I might try it on one more time. Just so my family can see it."

She motioned to the girl posse behind her.

The woman behind the counter turned an unhealthy shade of white.

"Right. Ms. Fairchild."

She cleared her throat, and Sidney wondered if she was about to vomit.

"Um... Sarah? Ms. Fairchild is here for her dress."

The designer and shop owner came rushing from the back with a strange look on her face.

"Hi!" Sidney greeted her in a voice full of optimism and roses. "Is my dress ready?"

Sarah reached out and took Sidney's hand.

"Ms. Fairchild. Yes! Your alterations are complete, and the gown is perfect."

"Yay! I can't wait to see it. I want to try it on for my aunt and cousins."

Sarah suddenly looked sick. "Ms. Fairchild, there is a... small... problem."

Sidney's stomach dipped.

Dread moved in like a rolling cloud of thunder.

"What? What's wrong? What happened?"

"Your gown was accidentally shipped to Thailand."

Sidney stared at her.

"I'm sorry. What?"

"Your gown," Sarah repeated. "It was accidentally shipped to Thailand."

Sidney closed her eyes.

She heard the words, but it wasn't computing in her brain.

She turned to Bree.

"What is she saying?"

"No." Bree shook her head. "We're not hearing her correctly. Let me handle this."

Bree stepped in front of Sidney still cradling Isla close, and stared at the dress designer.

"Sarah? That's your name, right?"

"Yes."

"Well, Sarah, Sidney would like to try on her wedding gown now. We're here because you said that this is the day and time that the alterations would be complete. So please take us back to the dressing area so that Sidney can try on her beautiful wedding gown now. Please."

"I would love to," Sarah said.

"Great. Thank you." Bree smiled at Sidney.

Sidney tried to smile back.

"But it was accidentally *shipped*. To Thailand."

The thunder broke loose, the storm exploding inside Sidney's head.

"No!"

Bree's voice was firm.

"How?" Sidney's was frantic. "How? How does a gown get accidentally shipped anywhere? Much less Thailand? *Thailand!*"

"I'm so sorry!" Sarah sounded as frantic as Sidney felt. "It was hanging next to a gown that was being shipped to Thailand for a customer having a destination wedding there this weekend, and your gown was shipped by mistake. We only noticed the mix up today when the destination wedding bride opened the package and had the wrong dress."

"What!"

"Believe me, *that* bride is no happier with me today than you are. I am so sorry! I've been on the phone all morning trying to make a miracle happen."

Tears stung the back of Sidney's eyes.

Could this day get any worse?

"This can't be happening. What am I supposed to do now? My wedding is in four days!"

"I'm so sorry!"

"Well, can you get it back from Thailand by then?"

"No. It took two weeks to get it *to* Thailand!"

"Oh, my God."

Was the room spinning?

"I think I'm going to faint."

Sidney stumbled over to the nearest chair and flopped down in it.

"Deep breaths, honey." Aunt Bobbie knelt next to the chair and patted her leg.

"I am so sorry!"

"Would you stop saying that and fix this mess!" Bree snapped at the woman.

"Yes! I absolutely intend to fix this. Yes."

Sarah came from around the counter and rushed over to Sidney.

"Ms. Fairchild, I'm going to make this right! You can pick out absolutely any dress in the shop. Completely free of charge! In fact... I'll eat the cost of the original gown too. Full reimbursement. New gown, plus any alterations. All totally free and ready in time for your wedding. Please, let me make this right for you!"

"That dress was one of a kind. You don't have another like it."

"No, I don't, but... but there has to be something here that you'll find just as beautiful. Oh, I know! That dress... the one you chose, it was part of a series that I called my tropical collection. All the dresses were similar in theme. I'll show you everything from that collection. Maybe you'll find one you love even more."

She snapped her fingers at her assistant and the girl scurried away.

"We will find you another dress, Ms. Fairchild. I promise!"

Tears hit Sidney's cheeks. She simply couldn't contain them anymore.

This was wrong.

Everything was going wrong, and she had no idea how to make it stop. She couldn't make Carlton go away and she couldn't magically make her wedding dress come back from Thailand. All she could do in that moment was sit and cry.

Bree suddenly knelt in front of her and gently dabbed at Sidney's damp cheeks with a tissue.

"Oh, Sidney. It's okay. It's all going to be okay. I promise, because you know what?"

Sidney looked at her and shook her head.

"Listen to me," Bree said, still dabbing at tears. "It's just a dress."

"It's not just a dress. It's my wedding gown!"

"Nope. It's just a dress, girlfriend. You have the most amazing man who loves you, and can't wait to marry you. And he is going to think you're an absolute dream when you come down that aisle, no matter what you're wearing. And here's the really good part, you know what else?"

"What?"

"You are an incredibly beautiful woman with a darling figure that looks great in everything!"

Sidney stared at her and then laughed through her tears.

Bree laughed too.

"There is no way my black girl booty looks great in everything. But I knew I was doing the right thing when I asked you to be my matron of honor. Thank you for fighting for me here, and for talking me down and making me laugh."

"Hey, my friend is about to become my family. You better believe I'm going to fight for you."

Sidney hugged her tight.

"Come on." Bree stood held a hand out to her. "Let's find you the perfect dress."

———

"I'm out. Going to lunch."

Tina Mayfield stood and walked away without another word, and Gerri watched her go. The woman hadn't said a single word to her since the unfair jab at Gerri and Gavin's relationship, and that was just fine with Gerri. It would be a shame to have to flatten her new partner on her ass, after all.

She tossed a pencil onto the desk and sat back in her chair.

The uncomfortable knot in her stomach squeezed tight.

Well, stewing about it wasn't helping.

She got up and walked through the busy detectives pit and into Gavin Hayes' office. He was hard at work and didn't even notice. When she closed the door he finally looked up and smiled at her.

That smile.

He'd always had a really great smile, but it was even more brilliant when it was meant just for her. She loved that about him.

In fact, there wasn't much she didn't love about him.

She walked over, and completely ignoring all the rules, stepped around his desk and slid fluidly into his lap.

The mild shock on his face made her smile.

His arms went around her without any prompting, even as he said, "You know, this probably is not a real good idea."

"I don't care. I need some Gavin time."

"You had Gavin time last night. And again this morning, as I recall."

The seductive grin on his lips and the tenderness in his deep voice stirred a longing in inside her, and made her want to burrow into his chest and stay there the rest of the day.

"I'm serious."

Their eyes locked and Gerri knew that he was studying her face, trying to get a read on what was wrong.

"I ran into Jo Haftel a little while ago in the pit," he said, referring to her new lieutenant. "She was singing your praises on getting a particularly skittish witness to talk. Apparently the DA says the case is in the bag thanks to you."

"Yeah."

"So, what's got you down, baby? You should be riding high right now."

"I know. And I was. I'm just sick of being the subject of rumors around here."

Gerri shrugged a shoulder and fiddled with the second button of his dress shirt.

"My new partner, Tina Mayfield?"

"What about her?"

"She sucker punched me with a comment about sleeping my way up the ranks."

She watched understanding bloom in Gavin's eyes.

"Okay. Now I get this mood you're in." He stared at her and sighed. "You know the rumors will die down. Eventually."

"It's been nearly two months now, Gavin. You'd think everyone would've found a much more salacious topic by now."

"Give it time, baby. They will lose interest. I promise."

"Well, that can't happen soon enough for me."

"So what did you say when Mayfield came at you like that?"

"Nothing. She didn't give me a chance. She just walked away. And I stood there feeling like an idiot. How can someone make you feel guilty when you didn't do anything wrong? How does that work?"

Gavin didn't answer that question, and Gerri snuggled closer to him.

"Tom Brewster came to see me yesterday."

That statement had her sitting up again and looking into his eyes.

"Captain Brewster?"

Gavin nodded. "He wanted to address the rumors."

"What? Why didn't you tell me this last night at dinner?"

"It just slipped my mind."

"Captain Brewster came to see you about the rumors and that slipped your mind? Well, what did he say? Was he angry?"

"Actually, he was very supportive."

"Really?"

"He said we did things the right way, you transferring divisions. Said the bottom line was that we acted responsibly and didn't jeopardize either of our jobs."

"So we won't be reprimanded?"

"Nope. Both of our records are clean. As clean as your conscious."

He grinned at her, and Gerri felt her smile splitting her face. Her record was clean. Declared clean by the Captain himself.

The knot in her stomach suddenly unraveled and she took a deep breath.

"Thank you for telling me this."

"You're welcome. Now go rub her face in it."

She laughed and kissed him.

———

The text had come at the most inconvenient of times. Right when Sidney was in the middle of feeling sorry for herself. But there was nothing she could do but suck it up.

Ronan, true to his word, had completed the false papers for Beth within his promised 24 hour timeframe.

Lucky for Sidney, she'd already dropped her aunt and cousins off at the hotel and was back at home, wallowing in wedding dress misery when the text came in.

She had dashed out of the house, happy she'd had the good sense to get the money from Beth beforehand. Ronan never gave her any time to stop by an ATM.

His text had said twenty minutes at the bench in the same park in Old Brooklyn where she'd met him the last time. She sat there now checking the time on her cellphone.

"An early bird ya were this time, lass."

He sat down beside her and placed a folded jacket on the bench between them. Sidney knew that the manilla envelop with the false papers was underneath it.

"Yeah, well, now I know how to get here."

She cut her eyes his way and looked him over.

He was wearing that same leather flat cap he wore over his closely cropped red hair, and his clothes were wrinkled like he'd let them sit in a laundry basket for too long.

"You know, you really should give a girl more than twenty minutes notice."

"Twenty minutes is plenty long enough from just about anywhere in the city."

"Not when you're unfamiliar with the city."

She sighed and looked out at the play equipment. A young mother watched as her little boy climbed on the jungle gym.

"Ya seem troubled, Sid the social worker. This charge got ya down?"

"This charge?" Sidney looked at him. "Oh. You mean the woman I'm helping."

"Aye. She been hurt bad?"

It wasn't Beth's plight that had her so down right now, but Ronan didn't need the details of her personal life, and he surely didn't need to hear about her wedding woes.

"Well, yes, she has been hurt very badly. And the asshole was molesting her child too."

"Agh!"

It was a disdainful hiss, and Ronan looked perturbed.

"There should be no mercy fer a man who could do such a thing to a child."

"I couldn't agree more."

Ronan stared at her for a moment.

"So who was the man that hurt you?"

Sidney turned and stared into his eyes.

"That is the reason ya do what ya do, isn't it? To help them run to freedom like you did."

"Careful, Ronan. I might begin to think you're one of the good guys."

He chuckled and picked up his jacket and pulled it on, leaving the manilla envelope where it sat.

Sidney grabbed the envelope and put it into her purse, replacing it with the envelope of money.

"Always a pleasure doin' business with ya, Sid."

"Likewise."

Ronan picked up the envelope of money and walked away.

Sidney watched the woman playing with her son and thought about all the absurdities of her day. The happy reunion with her family, spoiled by the intrusive appearance of her long lost father. The joy at picking up her wedding gown, ruined by the news that dress had been shipped halfway around the world. And now she sat in a park where she'd just paid a man one thousand dollars for illegal forged documents before heading home to make dinner for her police detective fiancé.

———

Isaac walked into the house at the end of the day, holding a small bouquet of Sidney's favorite roses — the kind that were the palest pink with darker pink centers.

"Meow."

Alfred Hitchcock greeted him at the door and Isaac bent over to give the fluffy cat a quick scratch hello.

The aroma of dinner cooking had his stomach growling.

"Isaac!"

Sidney set flatware and napkins on the table and stared, clearly delighted.

"What's the occasion?"

He smiled and kissed her lips, then handed over the flowers.

"Well, my intention was to cheer you up a little. I heard from Simon this afternoon that your wedding gown got lost by the bridal shop?"

She sighed. "Oh. That."

"What happened?"

"The bridal shop got my gown mixed up with another that was to be shipped to Thailand for a destination wedding. So, my beautiful wedding dress is off in a tropical paradise without me."

"Oh, no. Darlin' I'm so sorry."

"But how did Simon find out?"

"Beats me. Maybe one of your cousins told him. He was just calling to check in and let me know that he and your uncle and Jamal had a great time on the stadium tour. He wanted me to thank my dad. I told him he'd have ample opportunity to thank him himself this week."

"Yeah, I heard they all had a great time."

He watched Sidney sniff the roses, and he tried to gage her level of upset-ness. But she seemed to be taking it in stride. Either that or she was completely in denial somehow.

He followed her into the kitchen, where she pulled a vase from beneath the sink and began to fill it with water.

"So what happens now, Sid? With your dress? I mean, are they going to reimburse you for the dress so that you can buy another one somewhere else?"

"Actually, they offered to not only reimburse me, but also to give me another dress of my choice, free of charge."

"Really? Well, that's great."

"They know it was their mix up. I'm sure they don't want the bad press."

"So you took them up on it?"

"Of course."

Isaac watched her putting the roses into the vase one by one and wanted to scream. She was being so unanimated and not at all forthcoming.

"*And?* Did you find another dress?"

"I did."

She nodded nonchalantly, and he sighed.

"Well, you don't seem excited about it."

Sidney shrugged a shoulder and glanced at him.

"Aunt Bobbie and my cousins loved it. And Bree said she thought this new one was even more beautiful than the one I originally chose."

"But?"

"But I just really loved the other one."

Isaac reached out and gently pulled her into his arms.

"I'm sorry you can't have the wedding dress you wanted, darlin'. But I have no doubt in my mind that you are going to be stunning in this new dress."

She smiled at him. "Thank you."

He kissed her soft lips, letting his linger on hers for a moment. Then he flexed the fingers of his right hand and it started to tingle. He reached out toward the flowers lying on the counter and a single rose flew into his hand.

He grinned at her astonished expression and presented the rose to her.

"Show off." She smiled up at him.

"I've been practicing."

"So I see. It's going well?"

"It's going. Geneviève is thrilled," he said, referring to the woman who had become his psychic coach of sorts before he'd reconnected with his Grandad. "I'm just trying not to fear this particular ability."

"It still freaks you out?"

"Very much. I mean, it just shouldn't be possible, you know? Telekinesis is not real. People can't make objects move with only the power of their minds!"

Sidney smiled at him and Isaac rolled his eyes.

"Yes, I know. I just made a rose fly through the air. It's real."

He sighed and Sidney went back to arranging her roses in the vase.

He thought about the supposed curse on the Townsend family. And this stupid cursed gun.

"It's just like this shooting spree case. I talked to the SWAT commander today because he's like an amateur gun historian in his free time, right?"

"Yeah?"

"Well, he tells me there's all these stories in the gun world about a cursed Colt .45."

"Cursed?"

"Yeah. He gave me a file he's been compiling on the subject. And Sidney, I'm telling you... there are all these police reports and articles in this file that go back as far as 1942 talking about this Cursed Colt."

"What do the reports say?"

"They detail cases all around the country of mysterious shooting sprees where all the witnesses can clearly describe the gun used, but they have almost zero recollection of the shooter."

Sidney gave him a look.

"That sounds like your shooting spree case, baby."

Isaac sighed.

"I know it. But I'm having a hard time wrapping my head around the idea of a cursed gun being to blame here."

"And that's because you feel curses aren't real?"

"Well, they're not!"

"There was a time when you thought of your abilities as a curse."

"Yes, but I didn't mean that word literally. It was just a figure of speech."

"Do you still feel that way? About your abilities, I mean?"

Isaac sighed. How the hell was he supposed to answer that?

"I don't know, Sid. I mean, I still wish that I was just normal, you know?"

Sidney's luscious lips twisted into a smirk.

"Normal's overrated, baby."

"Maybe. But I just think that people use that word too quickly, or too recklessly, or something."

"Normal?"

"Curse."

He was so frustrated with this damn case. With both of them, in fact. He wanted to just forget about them, push them both off onto someone else, get married and fly away with Sidney to their honeymoon.

Hell, if they couldn't solve them before his wedding, they'd both be Pete's problem then. His partner would either solve them on his own, or they'd both still be staring at him once Isaac got back from his honeymoon.

He did not like that prospect at all.

"Telekinesis isn't real either, according to you. Yet, you possess that ability."

Isaac stared at her.

"Exactly. I don't know what to believe anymore. I don't know where to go from here. I can't take what I've learned to Lt. Hayes in any kind of serious discussion of this case. But we still don't have any suspects or even people of interest. None of the victims are connected in any way. It's so damn frustrating."

"I'm sorry, baby."

She stepped back into his arms, and Isaac hugged her, squeezing her close. He inhaled the sweet honeysuckle scent of her perfume and nuzzled her neck.

"I love holding you close like this."

"That is a very good thing, because I love when you hold me."

He nibbled on her earlobe and smiled when she shivered.

"So, we got time for a little somethin' somethin' before dinner?"

Sidney giggled, and the sound of it connected with his dick.

"What?"

"You are insatiable, Detective."

"Oh. Sorry, not sorry."

He slid his hand down to her ass and squeezed.

Sidney laughed and he bit her neck.

11

"Sterling is coming in today, isn't he?"

Sidney set her cup of tea down and looked at Isaac.

"Yes. Adam is supposed to pick him up at the airport this afternoon. I wonder if I should text and remind him about that?"

"Probably couldn't hurt," Sidney said, and took a bite of her breakfast.

She watched Ike pull out his cell and shoot off a quick text to his older brother and best friend. Then he took a huge bite of his waffle, causing her to grin. She loved his big appetite.

"So, what's on your agenda today, darlin'?"

"I'm actually hanging out with Aunt Bobbie, Erika, and Tameka today. They want to go shopping, and they want to see something cool about Cleveland since the boys got to do the stadium tour yesterday."

Isaac chuckled at that.

"So, first, I'm going to take them to Tower City Center so they can do a little shopping. And then I thought we'd hit the Rock Hall, because there's nothing cooler than that in my opinion."

The Rock Hall was short for the Rock and Roll Hall of Fame

and Museum, and Sidney loved the place. It was one of the places Ike had taken her when he was showing her all the things that made Cleveland special. Going through the museum was amazing, but just visiting the gift/record shop was an event in and of itself. Not to be missed by any serious music fan.

Isaac smiled at her. "Not even the lake?"

"Well, okay. The lake is pretty cool, but they'll see that on Friday at the wedding rehearsal."

Isaac was about to say something else, but his cellphone beeped, and he checked the text.

"Adam says he remembers about picking up Grandad. He also wants to know if we'd like to come to dinner at their place tonight. That way we can visit with Grandad, but he won't get overly tired with all the travel and whatnot."

"Sure. We can do that. What can we bring?"

Isaac's thumbs flew over the keys while she watched. Adam's response came fast.

"He says just us."

Sidney twisted her lips into a thoughtful pout.

"They're already doing so much for us right now; I wouldn't feel right going empty handed. Maybe I'll pick up some kind of dessert to take while I'm out today."

Isaac pushed away his empty plate and stood.

"I've got to get going. It's going to be a long day for me. I have to give my statement to IAB today over the whole Natalie Bains thing."

Sgt. Natalie Bains was a co-worker of Isaac's, and also the psycho bitch that had been harassing Sidney with bogus traffic stops complete with handcuffs and car searches. Not to mention slashing her tires and slipping live tarantulas in the mail for her to open.

Funny. She denied having any knowledge of those harrowing events, yet as soon as Ike confronted her and filed a formal complaint with Internal Affairs at work, the terror had stopped.

"Oh. I forgot about that."

"Yeah. Wish I could forget about it."

Bitterness dripped from Ike's tone like syrup, the southern twang thick as molasses.

"Well, be careful, baby. That woman has proven to be unhinged."

Isaac reached out and lifted her chin with a single finger.

"You be careful too. Driving around the city today, I mean. And if you need anything at all, call me."

Sidney grinned. The incident that had led to their meeting had been the direct result of her being completely lost in the city. A situation that had led to her witnessing a murder. She knew that Ike would always worry about her getting lost again.

"I won't get lost. I have that fancy GPS system you bought for me."

"Worth every penny to keep you safe."

He leaned down and kissed her, letting his tongue play with hers for several sweet seconds.

"I love you."

"I love you back."

He clipped his badge to his belt and gathered his gun. Then he winked at her and left.

Sidney polished off her tea and then got up to clear things away. When the doorbell rang she smiled and hurried to it.

What had he forgotten?

She opened the door with a smile.

Carlton Fairchild smiled back at her.

Her smile fell, pulled down by the bricks that landed in her gut.

"What are you doing here, Carlton?"

"I know that I don't have any right to expect you to call me Dad. But it sure would be nice."

The bricks in her stomach began to rumble. Was he serious?

"What do you want, Carlton?"

"To talk. I just saw your fiancé leave." He gestured to the street. "You two live together?"

"Do you have a problem with that?"

"No. I'm just trying to get to know you, Sidney. May I come in?"

Sidney stared at him. How had he even found out where she lived? And why did she feel so torn when she looked at him? She should hate him, shouldn't she? She should be as angry at the sight of him as Simon was.

Shouldn't she?

She sighed and stepped aside, hoping she didn't regret this.

He stepped inside and she led him to the combined living/dining room and began clearing away the breakfast dishes. Maybe if he saw how busy she was he would leave, and she wouldn't have to feel guilty about letting him in.

Why did she feel guilty about talking to him?

"Because you're worried that your mom would feel betrayed."

The truth of that thought slapped her in the face.

Carlton wandered over to the back wall near the kitchen where pictures hung like a mural, and stood studying them.

"I don't have a lot of time," she said, carrying dishes to the kitchen. "I'm meeting Aunt Bobbie and the girls at their hotel soon."

She didn't have to be there until ten, which gave her a couple of hours, but he didn't need to know that.

"You look happy in these pictures. Like you have a happy life."

Sidney walked back into the room and stared at him.

"I didn't. Have a happy life, I mean. Not until I came here to Cleveland and met Isaac. He turned everything around for me."

Carlton grinned at her. "You don't have to keep selling him to me. White cop or not, he obviously makes you very happy, and I can appreciate that."

They stared at each other for a beat.

"What are you doing here, Carlton? And I don't mean here at

my house. I mean here in Cleveland. Why did you come? You had to know that neither I nor Simon would be happy to see you."

Carlton's gaze dropped to his shoes for a moment.

"I admit I didn't exactly expect to be welcomed with open arms or anything. But I was surprised at Simon's viciousness. I didn't expect that."

"Can you blame him? From his point of view, you walked out on us at a time when you were still his hero. He loved you. He looked up to you. And then you left and never looked back. You broke his heart."

Carlton nodded and met her gaze.

"And what about from your point of view?"

A soft huff of breath escaped her.

"I was barely out of diapers. I've got maybe one or two memories of you from back then."

The words brought a flood of images to her mind like old home movies. Memories of events long forgotten.

Sitting on Carlton's lap sharing an apple.

Riding on his back while he pretended to be her pony.

Standing on his feet while he danced around the kitchen, smiling down at her.

Falling asleep in his arms with a thumb in her mouth.

She remembered that Daddy made her feel safe and loved.

She remembered having a daddy.

The realization burned in her belly like a fireball.

Tears stung her eyes.

But she would not give this man the happy reunion he wanted. She couldn't.

"There is no version of this where you don't look like a world class jackass for leaving. So, I hope you weren't expecting me to say something different."

"No. I guess not."

His voice was soft and full of emotion. He turned back toward the wall of pictures. He studied each of them, like he was hoping the framed snapshots would give him the information she wouldn't. He stared at them for so long that he startled her when he finally spoke again.

"She was so beautiful."

Sidney stepped closer, knowing that he was talking about her mom.

"You look just like her, you know?"

Sidney slowly shook her head.

"Not true. I didn't get her eyes. Neither of us did."

Carlton looked over at her. "You make it sound like I should apologize for leaving any part of me behind."

Sidney met his gaze, but said nothing.

Carlton shook his head.

"I don't know. Maybe I should. You and Simon... both of you got Dawn's wicked determination. And that fierce independent streak of hers. But it served you both well. I guess I should be grateful that the only thing either of you got from me was my eyes."

He turned and looked at her then, a tender smile crossing his lips.

"I can't believe you still have that thing."

"What thing?"

He motioned with a nod to her neck.

"The necklace."

Sidney's hand immediately went to the dainty gold necklace with the tiny cross charm she always wore. The one that had been her mothers.

"You've seen this before?"

"I gave it to Dawn for her birthday the year you were born. It was hot. Stolen, I mean."

Sidney stared at him, and he backtracked.

"I-I didn't steal it, but I bought it from someone who had..."

"I know what hot means," Sidney interrupted him with a curt snap.

"I only paid about sixty bucks for it. But she oohed and aahed like I'd given her diamonds or something."

Still fingering her precious necklace, Sidney stared at him, trying not to let this revelation ruin the necklace's significance for her.

"You gave her this?"

Carlton nodded. "We were together over eight years. But besides her wedding band, that was the only piece of jewelry I ever bought her." He looked Sidney in the eyes. "I was an asshole, Sidney. And Dawn was way out of my league from the start. She deserved much better than me. I knew it and she knew it too. That's why I left."

Sidney shook her head.

"Um mmm. No. You don't get off that easily. I understand relationships not working out. But I don't understand walking out on your children. Did you have to leave us just because you left her?"

The tears swimming in her eyes were mirrored by the tears swimming in his, and Sidney hated that she noticed his pain. She didn't want to acknowledge that he might be hurting too.

"No, you're right. I didn't. But I didn't understand that at the time. Sidney, I was young, and scared, and stupid. Back then... I didn't know how to stay in your lives. But by the time I grew up enough to figure that out, so much time had passed. And then Dawn was gone."

The tears hit his cheeks, and she watched him swipe at them with the back of his hand.

"I can only imagine the hell Bobbie would've given me if I'd tried to step back in and be a father then."

"You were a coward." Sidney wiped her own tears.

"Maybe so. Look, I don't expect you to understand. And I'm sorry that I'm not explaining myself very well."

"Oh, you're doing fine." Her tone was glib, and her anger was surfacing, her voice raised. "Why did you come here, Carlton? What do you want?"

"I've told you. I want to get to know you, all right? I just want to get to know my kids before I die!"

His words hung in the air above them.

Wait. What?

Was he serious?

Sidney stared at him in complete confusion.

"I'm dying, Sidney."

All the air left her lungs like they'd been flattened by a ten-ton weight.

"And I know that I don't have any right to ask you or Simon to give me the time of day. You both have every right to treat me like shit you scraped off the bottom of your shoe. But I'd like to get to know you both. Please?"

Mouth open, she stared at him while his words settled.

"What's wrong with you?"

"Apparently I have a tumor the size of a grapefruit wrapped around my brain stem. It's inoperable."

Sidney wiped more tears and turned away.

"How long?"

Carlton shrugged a shoulder.

"It could be three months, it could be three weeks." He tried for a grin. "Hell, it could be three days."

Sidney's head was throbbing. She wanted to tell him to stop talking, but at the moment she couldn't form words.

"Doctors aren't sure. They seem pretty certain I won't last a full year though. Hell, half a year. They didn't want me to leave, but I just couldn't see sitting in a hospital bed waiting to die if all I have left is a few months, you know?"

Sidney walked over to the sectional and flopped down with a sigh.

Carlton took a seat on the other side of it, watching her.

Alfred Hitchcock leapt to the couch with a meow, and settled in her lap. Absentmindedly, Sidney rubbed the cat's head.

"Sidney?"

She glanced in his direction, but she didn't make eye contact.

"Say something."

She took a breath and finally met his gaze.

"I don't know what to say."

"Fair enough." Carlton nodded. "Look, I'm not expecting anything from you. I just want the opportunity to sit, like this, and have a conversation. With Simon too. And I know you're getting married in a few days and you don't have a lot of time. I mean, I'm sure you've got a honeymoon trip or something. You could be gone a couple weeks or more. But, see the thing is... I-I just don't know if I'll still be around... you know... when you get back."

Sidney looked him in the eyes, still quite speechless. The look he gave her was apologetic.

"I'm not trying to play on your sympathies, I swear. I'm just being honest. Practical."

Sidney stared into space for a long time, just petting the cat and saying nothing.

Finally she took a deep breath and looked at Carlton.

"Would you like some coffee? Or breakfast? I made waffles."

Carlton gave her a grateful smile.

"Waffles and coffee sound great. Thank you."

12

"*A*ll right. Let's be safe out there."

Gavin dismissed them from the morning briefing and Isaac stood and moved over to the wall while everyone filed out of the room.

"You ready for this today?" Gavin asked him as they left the room.

"I'm more than ready to get it over with. I'm kinda sick of being questioned by IAB."

"I hear that."

"At least it's not my ass in the sling this time."

"Keep hold of that silver lining. How's the shooting spree case going? Any updates for me?"

They reached Gavin's office and Isaac sighed.

"Nothing solid. We're still at square one. There's just no connection between any of the victims. Still no ID on our shooter. I've got IT trying to enhance a shot of the license plate of a car we think the shooter sped off in after the last hit. Hopefully, they'll have something for us today. Pete will keep a look out for that call today while we're upstairs for the inquest."

"All right. Let's go get this over with."

They left his office and headed for the elevators.

Up on the sixth floor, they gave their names to the officer at the desk, who led them down the hallway to the room where they would each be questioned.

"Wait here. When they're ready for you, they'll come out to get you one at a time."

"Thank you." Gavin nodded and took a seat.

When the officer was gone, Isaac did the unthinkable and reached for the doorknob.

"What are you doing?"

Gavin's voice carried a warning, but it was already too late.

Isaac had the door opened a tiny crack.

He could see patrol officer Tammy Hunt being questioned. Could hear what they were saying.

"I was pissed, frankly," Tammy was saying. "I had no idea the person she'd asked me to pull over was the fiancée of Detective Sgt. Isaac Taylor."

"And what did you do when you discovered that?" Captain Norwall asked her. "Did you let Ms. Fairchild go?"

"Well, no, sir. I continued issuing the citation."

"So, first you agreed to pull someone over with the express purpose of giving them a hard time. Then, once you realized who the driver was, it didn't occur to you that perhaps Sgt. Bains had recruited you to help her harass a fellow officer?"

"Yes, something like that did occur to me. Which is why I was pissed at Sgt. Bains."

"But not pissed enough to cease abusing your power? Not pissed enough to cease issuing the bogus citation to Ms. Fairchild."

Isaac closed the door just as quietly as he'd opened it, then turned to Gavin.

"Did you hear that?"

"I did. Let's hope this means they're taking your grievances seriously."

They both took a seat on the bench by the door to wait, and Isaac drew his arms in tight toward his torso. Close to fifteen minutes later they saw Officer Tammy Hunt leave the room and walk briskly down the hall.

"She looks a little miffed," Gavin mumbled.

Isaac nodded, wondering what they said to her.

"Sgt. Taylor?"

He turned to see an aide standing in the doorway.

"They're ready for you."

"Okay."

Isaac stood and glanced down at Gavin, who gave him a silent nod of encouragement. He took a deep breath and followed the aide into the room.

It was the same room he'd been in a few months before when he was the one who'd been the focus of an IAB inquest. The three-man panel — Captain Norwall, Captain Bonner, and Sgt. Windsor — were seated at a long table at the front of the room, looking hella intimidating. The smaller, rectangle table facing them had just one chair — the chair Officer Hunt had just vacated.

Isaac took his seat in that chair and tried not to feel as though he were about to be put into the frying pan. After all, it was his formal complaint that had sparked this inquest.

"Good morning, Sgt. Taylor."

Captain Ted Norwall's tone said he was already tired of these proceedings and was in no mood for shenanigans.

"Good morning, sirs."

"We have a lot to get through this morning, Sergeant, so we'll jump right in."

"Yes, sir."

They began then, asking question after question about the incidents that led to the filing of the formal complaint. Isaac took them through everything — the complaint Natalie had filed against him, the verbal threats she'd made against Sidney, the recent string of terror Sidney had gone through, and the threats Natalie made when Isaac confronted her about it. He even threw in their screaming match in the middle of the pit for good measure.

The panel questioned him thoroughly about each incident, and Isaac found it difficult to read their faces. He had no idea how it was going. All he knew was that he'd been in the hot seat for a long freaking time.

They conferred quietly among themselves, and Isaac saw Captain Bonner glance his way and look him over as they whispered. Finally they leveled their gazes on him again.

"Sgt. Taylor, were you and Sgt. Bains ever romantically involved?"

The question came from Captain Bonner, and Isaac tried hard not to get indignant.

"No, sir, we were not."

"At no time did you date Sgt. Bains? Or engage in sexual relations of any kind with her?"

Isaac looked him in the eyes.

"I have never so much as flirted with Sgt. Bains, sir."

The three men looked at each other once again, and Isaac could tell a silent question was being asked. Finally Bonner shrugged a shoulder, and Captain Norwall turned back to Isaac.

"Sergeant, you've leveled some very serious accusations against Sgt. Natalie Bains here today," Captain Norwall stated. "Can you give us a reason for her alleged harassment? Why you and Ms. Fairchild? Why would she risk her career on such a foolish enterprise as harassing a fellow officer of the law?"

Isaac sighed and shook his head and thought about the question. He knew he couldn't tell them that Natalie was butt-hurt because he wouldn't give her any play. Even if it was the truth.

"Honestly, Captain, I don't know. I can't think of anything I did to offend her, or to step on her toes professionally in any way. She simply took an almost immediate dislike of me, and has been antagonistic toward me for the entire time I've known her. And when she learned that Ms. Fairchild and I were getting married, things took a sudden and very strange turn."

"And what do you hope to gain by filing this formal complaint with internal affairs? Is this a tit-for-tat situation, Sergeant? She filed one against you, so you filed one against her?"

"Absolutely not, sir. I filed a formal complaint because I felt I had no choice. She arranged for Ms. Fairchild to be stopped, handcuffed, and humiliated. That was bad enough. But then, she slashed the tires on Ms. Fairchild's car, and put a live tarantula in a package for Ms. Fairchild to open. The severity of the harassment was escalating quickly, and I felt I had to act. Both for Ms. Fairchild's safety, and for her peace of mind."

The panel seemed thoughtful as they took his last statement into account.

"Thank you, Sgt. Taylor. That'll be all."

"Thank you."

Isaac stood and followed the aide out of the room, where Lt. Hayes was called in.

"You look like you've just gone a few rounds with Ali."

Isaac let out a deep breath and looked at his boss.

"I feel like it too."

"Go on back to the pit. We can compare notes when I'm done."

Isaac nodded and Gavin entered the room. Then Isaac turned and headed for the stairs.

Gerri Miller sat at her desk going over paperwork and trying not to care that her new partner had barely said more than two words to her that morning. But it did tick her off though. How the hell were they supposed to gel as a team if Tina Mayfield wouldn't even talk to her?

She was about to open her mouth and ask her exactly that, when Lt. Jo Haftel walked up and handed Gerri a sheet of paper.

"What's that, Lieutenant?"

The level of jealousy in Tina's voice almost made Gerri grin, but she caught herself.

"Half an hour ago a patrol car in Central was flagged down by a 14-year-old who looked like she'd escaped from a war zone. Says she and two others have been kept chained in a cellar, but she couldn't say by who."

"Oh, man."

"She did lead them to the house she ran from though. FBI has been notified and they're en route, but patrol and detectives have the place under surveillance, just in case this guy tries to run."

"Good idea since his missing girl will undoubtedly spook him," Gerri said.

"Right."

"So, where do we come in, Lieutenant?" Tina asked.

"I want you two at the hospital on the girl." Haftel pointed to each of them in turn. "As you can imagine, she's extremely skittish. It's going to take a soft touch to get her to open up. That's why I'm giving it to you two."

She turned to Tina and grinned.

"Your new partner seems to have a natural knack for special victims. Kind of like someone else I know. So go do your thing."

Tina glanced at Gerri. "Yes, sir."

Gerri stood and headed for the stairs without glancing back to see if her partner was keeping up. Down in the lot, Gerri slid behind the wheel and Tina slammed the passenger side door when she got in.

As she drove, Gerri could feel Tina's angry gaze on her. Finally, halfway to the hospital, she couldn't take it anymore.

"You got something you want to say to me, partner?"

"Nope. Why do you ask?"

"I just feel you watching me, is all. Thought maybe you had something on your mind."

"Well, now that you mention it…"

Tina turned in her seat, and Gerri could tell she was settling in to tell her off.

"…I guess I am feeling some kinda way about being partnered with someone like you."

Gerri glanced over at her.

"Someone like me? You mean someone who had a successful two-year run in homicide before making a lateral move to special victims?"

Tina grinned. "Nah. I mean someone who doesn't mind finding success by laying on her back and spreading her legs for a man. I'm sorry, but this job is hard enough for those of us females who climbed up the right way. And all it takes is someone like you to make us all look bad in this boys club, you know?"

Gerri's whole body went rigid.

She clutched the steering wheel to keep from punching her partner.

Then she pulled the car to the curb and put it in park.

"What are you doing?" Tina practically yelled. "We have a victim to question. Proceed to the hospital!"

"Oh, I will." Gerri turned in her seat and glared at her. "But you and me are going to get a few things straight, right here, right now."

Warning flashed in Tina's eyes, but Gerri didn't give a damn.

"First, I am not some fresh-from-the-academy-rookie that you can talk down to whenever you feel like it. I've been on this job for seven years, two of those as a homicide detective. So if your intention is to intimidate me, you can give it up."

Tina crossed her arms and sneered at her.

"Second, I worked hard to earn the promotion to detective. I worked my ass off! And that had nothing to do with sex of any kind with anyone. It was just good old fashioned police work. Maybe you've heard of it."

"Are you finished?"

"No, I'm not. Third. Yes, I fell in love with my lieutenant. Deep, genuine, blissful, can't-live-without-you kind of love. But guess what? As soon as we realized our feelings for each other were real, I transferred out so that he would no longer be my commanding officer. We followed the rules, and yet the rumor mill just keeps on chugging out one lie after another. Got me feeling like I should be ashamed over things that never happened."

"All I know is…"

"You don't know shit! Captain Tom Brewster — head of the entire detective division — praised our forward thinking and adherence to policy on the matter by our decision for me to transfer. But hey, if you and all the other dumb asses in the pit still got a problem with it, by all means let me see what I can do to make you feel better!"

She stared Tina down and felt a small measure of satisfaction at the slightly stunned expression on her new partner's face.

Tina looked down and quietly cleared her throat.

"Well. I mean, if Captain Brewster doesn't believe all the rumors, I guess I shouldn't either."

Gerri huffed out a breath and rolled her eyes as she settled back in her seat and pulled the car back into traffic.

"So, I guess the rumor that someone supposedly saw the two of you going at it on Lt. Hayes' desk isn't true either?"

Gerri's mouth fell open.

"What! Who's saying that?"

Tina gave her a sheepish look and shrugged a shoulder.

"A lot of people."

"Well, it's not true. We have never had sex anywhere in that building!"

A big belly laugh erupted from Tina, and Gerri couldn't help herself. She laughed too and drove on. Maybe now that they'd cut through the bullshit, she and her new partner could start to gel.

———

Hiroshi Sato sped through the streets.

Well, he sped as much as the lunchtime traffic would allow — secure in the belief that if he were stopped, he could talk his way out of a ticket. He had a hot date, and nothing was going to keep him from it.

Okay, so it was only a date in his mind, but he wasn't about to be late.

He pulled up in front of the swanky condo building in the heart of downtown Cleveland and hustled inside, running nervous fingers through his coal-black hair and smoothing his hands down the front of his shirt and pants.

As soon as he hit the lobby, he knew the place was way out of his price range.

If, in fact, he actually had a price range.

But since he wasn't really in the market for a new apartment, it didn't matter.

This is stupid.

He knew it was stupid.

When he'd finally talked himself into dialing the number, he had every intention of simply asking the woman out on a date.

Coffee.

Or maybe dinner. He was going to do it.

But when she'd answered and he'd heard her voice, he kept saying all the wrong things. Somehow she got the idea that he was calling because he was looking for a new place. Every time she asked about what he was looking for in a new apartment, he couldn't correct her. He simply answered her questions.

So here he was, sailing into the high-priced condo's lobby like some big shot with luxury tastes.

He spotted her near the center of the lobby, texting on her cellphone. She was wearing a pale yellow dress and a matching pair of high heeled sandals that showed off an amazing set of legs and made it difficult for him to think. Her dark brown hair fell past her shoulders with fashionable bangs hanging over her pretty brown eyes.

She looked up and smiled as he approached.

"There you are, Dr. Soto. So nice to see you again!"

"Ah, again? You remember meeting me before?"

"Of course. At Sidney and Isaac's housewarming party. I remembered the minute you said your name on the phone when you called."

"Oh."

Floored.

She remembered him, and he was floored by that. That was a good sign, right?

"Hey, I'm sorry I'm late. I couldn't scoot out of the lab on time."

"No problem. A medical examiner's work is never done, I suppose."

"No. Not in this town."

"Right this way, doctor."

She led him over to the elevators, and a weird swirling sensation took over in his abdomen, and Hiroshi smiled. He couldn't believe she remembered meeting him at Ike and Sidney's housewarming party. That knowledge made him ridiculously happy.

"Just Hiroshi, please. And it's great to see you again too. I was afraid you wouldn't remember me at all."

"How could I forget? You're Isaac's *other* Asian friend. It's probably a good idea for us to compare notes every once in a while, right?"

Hiroshi laughed, remembering the horribly bad joke he'd made the first time they'd met.

"Are you ready to see the condo?"

"Oh. Ah, sure."

"Let's head up."

She pushed the elevator button and the doors opened immediately. When they stepped inside, she whirled around, flipping her hair over her shoulder and giving Hiroshi a sweet whiff of her tropical flowery perfume. The scent of it made him want to fall at her feet.

Everything about her made him want to fall at her feet.

She was stylish, smart, funny, and gorgeous. All the things he'd ever wanted in a woman, and here he was too terrified to man-up and ask her out like a normal guy. No, he had to go through this elaborate ruse just to see her again.

Oh, God.

He was going to have to see a dozen places and actually buy a condo just to get to know her, wasn't he?

On the tenth floor, they got off and he followed her to the door of an empty unit and waited for her to unlock the place.

When they entered, the exposed brick walls, the beautiful crown molding, and the sunlight streaming in through the windows was mighty impressive. Hiroshi actually found himself picturing his stuff in this amazing place.

"Wow."

"Right?" Miku beamed at him. "On the phone, you mentioned condos with a loft feel, and..."

She spun around, gesturing at the open floor plan.

"This one is pretty spectacular, don't you think?"

"Yeah, it is. It's great."

Miku stopped and smiled at him.

"Now, we didn't talk much about your price range on the phone, so I brought you here first just to give you an idea of what's out there. This, of course, is top of the line at $399,900. Two bedrooms, two baths and over fourteen hundred square feet. And, naturally, some of that price is paying for the location, so once we pinpoint the amenities you're looking for in a place I'm sure I'll be able to find you something you'll love."

"Uh huh."

Hiroshi swallowed and wandered around the place wondering how he was going to dig himself out of this hole that was getting deeper by the minute.

"So, let's talk about your price range for a minute. I'm sure you've given that some thought?"

"Ah... yeah. I... actually haven't gotten that far yet."

"Oh. Well, you give it some thought then. That's really the most important starting point for me as a Realtor. Give me a price range and maybe a list of things you really want your new home to have, even if it's just a certain feeling you're looking for. And then I can get to work hunting for your perfect place."

"Yeah. No, that makes perfect sense."

He was an idiot.

She was going to think he was an absolute idiot, and she'd be right.

"Dr. Soto?"

"Hiroshi."

"Hiroshi?"

"Yes?"

"You're not really in the market for a new place, are you?"

Oh, here it comes.

Flames lit up his cheeks.

He could feel it.

Had he ever been more embarrassed in his life?

"Not really, no."

"Then why are we here?"

He sighed, and the weight of ten worlds sagged down his shoulders.

"We're here because I was too chicken to ask you out over the phone the other day. I didn't think you'd remember meeting me at Ike and Sidney's housewarming party, and I didn't want to come off as creepy or anything. Although, I'm sure this little ruse hasn't helped in that regard either, has it?"

To his astonishment, Miku laughed at him.

"Actually, I don't find your behavior creepy at all."

"You don't?"

"No. I think it's kind of sweet."

"Really?" He could not have stopped the big stupid grin on his face if he'd tried. "Boy, you really would've loved it if I'd kept asking to see more places just so I could hang out with you again."

"I'd have been even more thrilled when you bought a place just to make me happy. But I guess that's not going to happen now."

Hiroshi laughed, and she smiled. He really did love her sense of humor.

"Well, since we're not looking at condos today, how'd you like to buy me lunch, handsome?"

Hiroshi grinned. She thought he was handsome.

"I would love that!"

13

*I*saac sat at his desk, plodding his way through paperwork and wondering what was taking Lt. Hayes so long. He glanced down at his watch. It had been over a half hour since IAB had sprung him. Over half an hour since Gavin's questioning had begun. He knew that the complaint he'd filed against Natalie carried serious weight, and he was thankful that IAB was being so thorough, but man, it was starting to rattle his nerves. And he wasn't even the one being investigated.

He pushed it aside and focused on his very mundane task. The extra paperwork was the part of his new sergeant duties that he disliked the most. In fact, it was the only bad part he'd found so far.

For the most part, he could honestly say that he was enjoying his promotion to sergeant. He liked the higher rank, and not just because it had come with a small raise. He liked the fact that he was second in command of the homicide division, and that Lt. Hayes laid more responsibility at his feet.

"Hey, you're back."

He looked up just as Pete took his seat at the desk across from his own.

"Yep. Been back for a while now. Figured you were out to lunch."

"Yeah. If I'd known you were out I would've brought you a sandwich or something."

"Don't sweat it. I ate some junk food out of the vending machine."

"So, how'd it go?"

Pete looked eager, and Isaac didn't have to ask what he was talking about.

"About as well as it could, I suppose. They kept me in there for close to an hour."

"Really?"

"Yep. Hayes is still up there now."

Pete started to say something when Isaac's cellphone beeped, indicating a new text. He picked it up and read it.

"It's Hiroshi. He says he has something for us."

"One of our shooting spree vics?"

Isaac shrugged a shoulder and stood.

"I don't know."

They left the pit and headed down two flights of stairs and through the breezeway to the ME's office, and into the lab.

Hiroshi looked up and smiled when they entered.

"Guess who had lunch with the most beautiful Real Estate Agent in the city today?"

Isaac fought the eye roll and grinned instead.

"And how is the lovely Miku Barlow these days?"

"She's fantastic! Best first date I've ever had in my life. The woman is brilliant and funny, and we're going out again tomorrow night."

"Way to go, man."

Pete and Hiroshi high-fived.

This eye roll Isaac didn't fight.

"Congratulations. I hope it works out for you. Why'd you text me?"

Hiroshi chucked a thumb Isaac's way and shot Pete a look.

Pete twisted his lips and nodded in agreement of Hiroshi's unspoken rebuke.

"I called you down because I did some digging."

Hiroshi walked over to his work station, beckoning Isaac and Pete to follow.

"At your request, I sent a sample of Gregory Townsend's blood to an outside lab to check for lesser known common toxins."

"Oh, this is about our family curse case." Pete sounded mildly surprised. "Sweet."

"And what'd you find?" Isaac asked.

Hiroshi pulled a few papers from the printer and handed them over.

"Report shows lethal levels of oleandrin and neriine."

"Come again?"

Hiroshi grinned. "They're two very potent chemicals that are found in the oleander plant."

Isaac glanced at Pete, who shook his head.

"What's an oleander plant?"

"I had to look it up too. It's a shrub that produces pink or purple flowers. Apparently it's very common in gardens around the country. But every part of it — from the roots to the flowers — is poisonous when ingested. Basically, a large enough dose will seriously wreak havoc on your heart rhythm."

"So, you're saying that Townsend was poisoned?"

Isaac smiled when he asked the question. He couldn't help it. But the fact that there was no curse at play here made him almost giddy.

"That's exactly what I'm saying."

"But wait a minute," Pete held up a hand. "If he was poisoned, does that mean there's no family curse?"

"Damn right, there's no curse," Isaac repeated. "I'm betting there never was."

"Well, I can't help you with the other men in this guy's family who died young. But Gregory himself was simply poisoned."

"And this oleander stuff. I take it doctors don't normally test for that?"

"Unless there's some reason to test for less common toxins, most ME's wouldn't bother."

Isaac looked at Pete again. "Well, it looks like we got us a homicide here after all." He raised the toxicology report and grinned at Hiroshi. "Thanks for this, man. And congratulations again on the date thing. You should bring Miku to the wedding."

"Thanks. I think I will."

As they left the lab, Isaac was still grinning.

"You know, Ike, it occurs to me that just because Gregory Townsend was poisoned, that doesn't mean he wasn't the victim of a family curse."

Isaac stared at him. "What? How do you figure?"

"Well, the curse just says that all the men of the family will die young, right?"

"Supposedly."

"Okay. So it doesn't say anything about the manner of those deaths. Just that they'd die young."

Isaac's giddiness was quickly evaporating. He stopped walking and looked at his partner.

"What's your point, Pete?"

Pete smiled and kept walking.

"I think I just made it."

Isaac sighed. "Curses are bullshit," he mumbled, and followed Pete back up to the detectives section.

He reached his desk at the same time Gavin did.

"Hey, Lieu. How'd it go?"

Gavin placed his hands on his hips.

"Not too bad I don't think. They started out asking me about the incident two months ago when you and Bains were screaming at each other out here."

Isaac took his seat.

"You mean the day she got her notice that I'd filed a formal complaint with IAB about her harassing Sid and me."

"Right. Since I broke up that altercation, they had a lot of questions about that. Then they asked me if I knew anything about the feud between the two of you."

"What'd you tell them?"

Gavin shrugged a shoulder.

"The truth. That I was aware of some animosity between you, but that I have no idea where it originates from. They asked if I had any specifics I wanted to share. So I told them about how she got this ball rolling by anonymously filing a complaint against you for questionable behavior with a witness several months back, and that it seemed like a blatant case of jealousy to me."

"You said that?"

"I sure as hell did. She started these games. It's about time she gets called out for it."

"Well, do you know if they've made a ruling yet?"

"Yep. Inquest is being held over for a hearing. Natalie is being put on administrative leave with pay until the outcome."

A lightning bolt struck Isaac's core.

"You're shitting me."

Gavin shook his head. "No, I am not."

"Holy crap," Pete mumbled.

"You know what this means, right?" Gavin looked Isaac in the eyes.

"What's that?"

"That you and Sidney are going to have to be extra vigilant. Because something tells me Natalie Bains is going to see this as all your fault."

Isaac rocked back in his chair and sighed.

"Probably so. Thanks for the heads up, Lieu. And for the support."

"Always."

Gavin headed for his office, and Isaac sat there, stunned.

"Wow." Pete sounded just as dumbfounded. "I didn't really expect them to go to a full blown hearing."

"Yeah, me neither."

"This could seriously impact her career, Ike. Even end it."

Isaac slowly nodded. He never intended to hurt her career in any way. Of course, he'd never intended for Sidney to become the focus of her sadistic games either. No one was going to mess with Sidney and get away with it. Not on his watch.

"If she didn't want me to fight back, she shouldn't have started this war."

"I hear you. But Lieu's right, you know? Natalie is totally going to see this as all your fault."

"I know."

"If you need any help... you know, patrolling your street, watching your house, that kind of thing. Just let me know."

"Thanks. But you have enough on your plate right now. In fact... if you or your mom need anything. Anything at all. You let me and Sid know."

"Thanks, man."

Isaac got back to his paperwork then, only to be interrupted again ten minutes later.

"Hey, isn't that your FBI friend?" Pete asked with a lift of his chin.

Isaac looked up to see Special Agent Emmett Fox stroll from the elevators over to Lt. Hayes' office and knock on the door.

"Yeah, that's him."

He could hear the curiosity in his own voice.

They watched the door open, and Gavin shook Fox's hand and closed the door behind him.

"I wonder what that's about." Pete sounded just as curious.

"I don't know."

He turned back to his paperwork, but before he could pick up the pen, Gavin poked his head out of the office door.

"Taylor!"

He motioned Isaac over with a nod of his head.

"Well, I guess I'm about to find out."

Pete grinned, and Isaac stood and marched to Gavin's office, closing the door behind him.

"Emmett." He greeted the agent with one of those what's-up nods.

"Hey, Ike."

"What are you doing here?"

"Agent Fox says he has some important information that he feels we need to know." Gavin crossed his arms and sat on the edge of his desk.

They both gave him their full attention.

"I'm coming to the two of you because I've never dealt with Lt. Mike Dunbar before. I don't know what the man's about and frankly, the nature of this information makes it uncertain who to trust." Emmett looked Isaac in the eyes. "I do, however, trust you."

Isaac nodded.

"Well, that's mutual. But what exactly are we talking about?"

Emmett took a breath and addressed Gavin.

"Ike is aware of this, Lieutenant, but to quickly catch you up... the FBI has been investigating Boston Martelli for nearly two years. We're close to making a RICO case against him."

"Boston Martelli? On what grounds?"

Boston Martelli was a wealthy businessman who had his hands in several different ventures in and around the Cleveland area. The man was into everything from real estate to importing/exporting and even finance. Rumors had been floating around law enforcement circles for years that Martelli was tangled in deep with organized crime, but nothing had ever been proven.

"Racketeering. Drug and human trafficking. Murder. Those are just the highlights."

Gavin looked at Isaac.

"And you knew about this, Ike?"

"Well, no, sir. Emmett only mentioned it to me in passing a couple of months ago. I knew they were investigating the Martelli operation, but I had none of the details until now."

"No, it wasn't in an official capacity that I mentioned it to him," Emmett spoke up, and then appeared to get slightly flustered. "You see, sir, I've been dating Sgt. Taylor's sister, and..."

Gavin waved an impatient hand.

"Understood. Continue, please."

"Right. Well, some information has come to my attention, and I thought someone here at CPD should have a heads up."

"What's going on, Emmett?"

"Our man on the inside of Martelli's inner circle just fingered a Sgt. Natalie Bains as one of Boston Martelli's close associates."

They say lightning doesn't strike the same place twice.

But Isaac's system didn't get that memo.

Struck to the core, like scorched earth.

"A little digging into her led me here to the 3rd precinct," Emmett explained. "I understand Bains is the head of your narcotics special task force?"

Isaac and Gavin looked at each other, and Isaac knew that Gavin must have recognized the mild shock on his face because he spoke up when Ike couldn't.

"Um, yes. She is the head of the narcotics special task force, and Lt. Mike Dunbar is her immediate supervisor."

Emmett nodded. "That would track with what our man is telling us."

"Which is?" Isaac asked, finally able to speak.

"That Bains is one of Martelli's key enforcers on the street. She and her crew — who I'm assuming are other task force members — muscle the area big time dealers into falling in line with Martelli. Basically paying him to keep their operations going. They either get on the Martelli train or they're done. Permanently, if you get my drift."

"I don't believe I'm hearing this," Gavin said.

"Our source says Bains was in the process of bringing Nacio Rivas-Solis into the Martelli organization when he was killed, by you, Ike."

Isaac huffed out a soft breath.

He could feel his blood pressure rising.

"Then it's true. Natalie gave up the safe house to that drug-dealing, murdering son of a bitch. She gave up Sidney's location to that prick and almost got her killed. Twice!"

"Yeah, but you got him in the end, Ike. Don't forget that."

Gavin held his gaze, and Isaac knew his boss was trying to calm him down.

"You taking out Rivas-Solis apparently set Bains back a bit with Martelli," Emmett continued.

"What do you mean?"

"Our guy says Martelli doesn't like screw ups. Rivas-Solis' organization was a thriving one, and Martelli was looking forward to the revenue it was set to bring in once it fell under his umbrella. But his unexpected death put an abrupt end to that, and it made Bains look bad in Martelli's eyes for awhile. She's been scrambling ever since to make up for it. Our guy says she worked her way into Martelli's bed to help smooth things over."

Isaac shook his head and turned away, pacing the office like a caged tiger.

His right hand began to tingle, his avenging telekinesis begging to be unleashed.

But he balled his fist, took a deep breath, fought hard to rein it in.

"This is unbelievable." Gavin shook his head. "What do you want us to do with this information, Agent Fox?"

"I'm not entirely certain. I simply felt that someone here at the 3rd precinct should know what's coming down the line. When we do lower the boom on Boston Martelli, chances are Sgt.

Natalie Bains and a few of her team mates will be going down with him."

Isaac, still pacing and fuming, glanced over at Gavin.

Gavin sighed. "As of about an hour ago, Sgt. Bains was put on administrative leave with pay pending an upcoming IAB hearing."

"Really? Why?"

Gavin proceeded to explain the situation to Emmett while Isaac paced and tried not to picture himself exacting revenge on that poisonous snake of a bitch.

"Wow."

It was Emmett's only response once Gavin had brought him up to speed.

Gavin looked at Isaac.

"You know, Ike... this might go a long way to explaining why Natalie suddenly got so hung up on you and Sidney in the first place. I believe she was initially jealous of your relationship. But she thought she could take care of that by giving up the safe house and having Sidney killed."

"As if Sidney being gone would make me look her way."

Isaac made no effort to hide the vile bitterness in his voice.

"But when that didn't work," Gavin continued, "and you ended up killing Rivas-Solis, it jeopardized her standing with Martelli, and *that* really pissed her off. Probably jeopardized her cut of whatever money Martelli promised her too."

Isaac stopped pacing and Gavin's take on things clicked in his mind.

"That's why she's been coming at me and Sidney the way she has. We got in her way. Threatened her extra income."

"Exactly."

They were all silent for a moment. Then Isaac turned to face them both.

"So. Do we take this info to Lt. Dunbar, or keep it to ourselves and wait for the fireworks?"

"As tempting as that sounds," Gavin said, "I think we have to take it over Dunbar's head. I need to call in Captain Brewster. Probably Chief Branson as well."

Gavin turned to Emmett.

"You got time to hang around for this meeting, Agent Fox?"

Emmett shrugged a shoulder. "By rights, I probably should've taken it to the top myself, so sure. I'll stay."

Gavin nodded and then walked around his desk and picked up the office phone to call the Captain and the Chief.

Emmett turned to Isaac.

"Listen, Ike, while we've got a second... I hope you don't mind, but Emily asked me to be her plus one for your wedding."

Despite his still frothing anger, Isaac managed a small hint of a smile.

"Oh, did she?"

"Yeah. I hope that's okay with you."

"The more the merrier. In fact, why don't you come to the bachelor party too? I'll add you to the guest list."

"I'd be honored."

"Brewster and Branson will be right down." Gavin rejoined them with a grave expression. "I don't expect this to be fun."

Twenty minutes later, Isaac sat in a bull session with Gavin, Emmett, Captain Tom Brewster, and Police Chief Luther Branson, who was every bit as appalled and blown away by Emmett's information as they had been.

"The scandal this creates is going to blow through our narcotics division like a shock wave. And the bitch of it all is that I don't even know if we'll still have a narcotics division when this is over," Branson said. "Is it just the task force that's corrupt, or is it the whole damn department? And is Dunbar clueless or complicit?"

"I'm afraid I don't know the answer to that, Chief. Which is why I brought this information to Lt. Haynes and Sgt. Taylor. Because I've worked with them before on two separate cases and I knew I could trust them."

Branson nodded, but he looked utterly disgusted. Isaac couldn't blame him.

"Yeah, well, you should've brought it directly to me."

"I do apologize, sir."

The tension in the room was overpowering. Isaac could feel it straining against the walls, it was so thick.

"We have to share this knowledge with Internal Affairs." Captain Brewster glanced around at them. "Since Bains' inquest was just held over for a hearing today, and this new information seems to be connected, they'll need to know."

"Yes, they'll need to know. I'll speak with Bob Mason myself," Branson said, referring to the lieutenant over the Internal Affairs Bureau.

"That'll be the end of her career in law enforcement," Gavin stated.

"Yes, it will. And rightfully so, it seems."

"Ah..." Emmett held up a finger and looked at Chief Branson. "I'm going to need you to hold off on that."

"What? Why?"

"I came here as a courtesy, sir. But this is still a federal investigation. Natalie Bains' connection to Martelli cannot be revealed before we're ready to make a move on him. If you take this information to Internal Affairs you'd be jeopardizing a two year investigation, not to mention the lives of the two men we have inside Martelli's organization."

"So what the hell are we supposed to do?" Captain Brewster blurted out. "Just let a dirty cop continue to operate in my detectives division?"

"For a little while longer, yes!"

Emmett's voice bounced around the office, and he glared at Brewster.

Isaac had never heard Emmett so much as raise his voice before, but the agent's cool had definitely snapped. Both his tone and his demeanor said he meant business.

The tension swelled, making the room feel like a powder keg.

"How long is a little while longer?" Brewster all but yelled.

"I don't know, Captain. As long as it takes."

"You Fed boys. Always thinking your cases are more important than the local ones."

"I assure you, I have nothing but respect for local law enforcement, Captain. But I'm going to need your cooperation on this. Either you give it willingly or I'll have no choice but to charge you with obstruction of justice in a federal case."

"You son of a..."

"Tom, back down!" Chief Branson snapped.

Brewster, now red in the face, clamped his mouth tight, and Isaac was thankful the situation hadn't come to blows.

"You know as well as I do that this is the Fed's call." Branson continued to chastise the Captain. "IAB will get this information. But they'll get it at the appropriate time. Like I said, I'll speak to Lt. Mason myself and see if I can get him to push Sgt. Bains' hearing out a couple of months."

He looked at Emmett.

"Would that give the FBI enough time, Special Agent?"

"It should."

"All right. Then this matter is settled."

"Thank you, Chief. If it'll help when the shit finally does hit the fan, I'll make sure the press knows that this department — namely you and Captain Brewster — worked very closely with our investigation to help bring down Martelli's empire and help weed out the corruption within the CPD detective division."

Tom Brewster grunted at that offer.

Chief Branson smiled.

"More of my campaign to flush out corruption and improve the level of policing here in Cleveland." Branson used air quotes for that slogan. "That's what we called it after ex-Deputy Chief Jay Schiffer was apprehended for his role in the Lullaby Murders."

"That's what they called it, sir." Isaac confirmed. "The media ate it up."

Brewster grunted again, still clearly unhappy with the situation, but Isaac knew the Captain to be a staunch team player. He would do what his Chief ordered him to do.

A knock sounded at the office door and Pete Vega poked his head inside.

"Sorry to interrupt, sirs, but we've got reports of a possible jumper off the Detroit-Superior Bridge. Plates on the vehicle at the scene match the plates on the video footage we got from the strip mall shooting yesterday."

Isaac drew in a deep breath.

"Well, sounds like our shooter might be ready to confess."

Gavin pointed a finger at him.

"You just make sure you get him off that bridge in one piece. He doesn't get to take the easy way out after what he's done."

Isaac nodded and stood. He turned to Agent Fox.

"Emmett, thanks again for bringing this info to us."

"Of course."

"Captain. Chief." Isaac nodded to each of them before he headed for the door.

"Sergeant."

He closed the door behind him and followed Pete through the pit.

"What the hell was that powwow about? It looked intense."

"I'll fill you in on the way."

They rushed out of the station and to their car. On the ride to the bridge, Isaac told Pete about the meeting with Agent Fox and Captain Brewster, stressing the need for secrecy.

"Damn. So you finally got confirmation that Natalie Bains is our department leak."

Pete sounded somewhat shellshocked, and Isaac supposed he couldn't blame him. It was a hell of a thing to try and wrap the head around.

"Well, she's definitely the one who gave up the safe house all those months ago. Still can't say for certain that she's the leak around here though. Could be two different things."

"My money's on her." Pete said. "Hey, you remember that half a million that went missing after that failed drug bust where Officer Tim Harold was killed?"

"Yeah. What about it?"

"Well, from what you just told me, doesn't it kind of sound like that money may have gone straight into Boston Martelli's coffers?"

Isaac glanced over at him and then back to the road.

"It does at that. You know, at the time, I was just thinking that she swiped that money for herself. But if what Agent Fox says is true — and we have no reason to believe otherwise — then yeah. That money was most likely always intended to go to Martelli. And Natalie saw to it that it got there."

They were both silent for a while, and Isaac's mind ticked away, connecting the dots.

"You know, it also makes me wonder now if Tim Harold was a weak link in her chain."

Pete nodded.

"You mean like maybe he wasn't willing to go along with the rest of his task force buddies and get paid to do her bidding?"

"That. Or maybe he was getting shaky. Maybe he wanted out. And, of course, by that point they couldn't just let him out because he knew way too much. So Natalie, or one of her guys killed him and claimed he was a casualty of the so-called failed drug bust."

Pete shook his head. "Man. Sounds like Sgt. Bains is way more crooked than we originally thought."

"Doesn't it though?"

They pulled up behind a black and white cruiser and the would-be jumper's vehicle at the bridge. When they go out of the car, the first thing Isaac saw was two uniformed officers attempting to talk the man back from the railing.

"Do we have a name on this guy yet, Pete?"

"Yeah. Plates came back to a Raymond Kotkin."

He and Pete moved forward slowly. The last thing they wanted to do was spook this guy.

One of the officers turned and made eye contact, and Isaac could see the relief pour over his face. He didn't want to be responsible for this guy taking a deep dive.

Isaac stepped past him and inched closer to the railing. Their jumper was standing on the outer side of it, staring down at the water.

"I have to. I know what I have to do now."

"Raymond?"

The man glanced in Isaac's direction, but he didn't look directly at him.

"Can I call you Raymond? Or maybe you like Ray better?"

There was a pause, and the man watched the water like he was waiting for it to dance.

"I prefer Raymond."

His voice was hollow, but at least he was talking. That was a start.

"Okay, Raymond. I'm Isaac. But you can call me Ike if you want to."

Isaac carefully inched even closer. He glanced down at the rushing water of the Cuyahoga River. The sound of it roared in his ears.

"So what are you doing up here, Raymond? If you're not careful, you might slip and fall. You don't want to end up down in the water, do you?"

"I have to."

"Why? Why do you have to?"

"Because I hurt them."

The man was distraught. He shook his head, tears flowing from his eyes.

"I didn't mean to. I didn't want to hurt all those people."

"Then why'd you do it, Raymond? Why did you shoot those people?"

"I didn't want to, I swear I didn't. I'm a good person. But I couldn't get the voice of the gun out of my head. It made me do it. It made me."

The voice of the gun?

Like the gun actually talked to him?

Was this guy for real?

"Raymond, where is the gun now?"

Raymond pointed down to the river.

"I had to. I had to get rid of it. It wouldn't let me stop, it just kept pushing and pushing. So I had to get rid of it. I thought about dumping it in the lake, but... well, this was closer."

Isaac turned to Pete.

"Get on the horn and get some divers out here to search the river to try and locate the gun. Then call for a bus. Tell them he'll need a mental work up."

"Got it." Pete hustled away pulling out his cellphone.

Isaac turned back to Raymond. He had to get this man off the edge of the bridge.

He flexed his right hand.

If ever there was a time when he needed to have command of this crazy telekinesis shit, it was now. Only Isaac had no clue if he could summon it like that. Moving a single rose across the counter into his hand was one thing. But could he flip a grown man backwards over the railing onto the safety of the bridge? Or maybe he could hold the man in place where he stood long enough to grab him and pull him in.

Only one way to find out.

He flexed his hand again, but nothing happened.

He shook it, and flexed again.

Nothing.

Shit!

His grandad would know how to do this.

Raymond's foot slid closer to the edge.

"Raymond. Let's take a step back and talk a minute, okay? Tell me what the gun was saying to you."

"I have to do this. I have to."

Raymond let go of the railing and took a step toward oblivion.

"*Nooo!*"

Isaac lunged forward, right hand extended, tingling.

For a split second, Raymond was suspended in mid-air.

The weight of him had Isaac groaning.

He grabbed the back of the man's jacket and yanked.

Raymond fell backward over the railing and landed on the bridge.

Isaac stumbled forward and caught himself from falling on top of the man.

"Ike!"

Pete and the two uniformed officers came running.

Isaac grabbed the railing to steady himself. Panting, he watched the two uniformed officers get Raymond Kotkin cuffed and on his feet.

"You all right, man?"

Pete sounded concerned, and Isaac nodded.

"I'm fine. I thought I lost him."

"It looked like you had. I don't know how you did it, Ike. I mean, he stepped off the bridge. How you caught him and threw him back over the railing I'll never know."

Isaac took several deep breaths and walked over to Raymond.

"Raymond. Why'd you do it? Why did you shoot all those people?"

"The gun made me do it. It told me to. I... I had to. The gun it... it made me."

Isaac shook his head. Everything this guy was saying lined

right up with the things he'd read in the research file Franklin Ross had given him on the Cursed Colt.

"Where did you get the gun, Raymond?"

"I found it. I saw it sparkling in the sun and picked it up."

"Where'd you find it?"

"I..." Raymond paused and appeared to think about it. "I... I saw it sparkling in the sun, so I picked it up. It was beautiful."

Raymond started describing the gun in great detail, and Isaac sighed. He motioned for the officers to get him into the cruiser.

"You believe him, Ike?"

Still shaking his head and breathing heavy, Isaac put his hands on his hips.

"This one played out exactly like all the other cases in that file Ross gave me."

"Does that mean you're changing your mind about curses? You believe the Cursed Colt really exists?"

"Let's just say I'll be surprised if the divers actually pull that gun out of the river."

14

*L*ater that evening, Pete sat on the sidelines with Jada while they watched Mateo and Charlie battle it out on some arcade game with flashing lights that were giving him a slight headache.

These group outings had become something of a standing date for the four of them. Wednesday nights they'd get the boys together and go for burgers or pizza, always followed by a movie or a trip to the arcade.

Mateo and Charlie had come to look forward to it, and Pete was thrilled that the two of them got along so well. Somewhere over the past two months Charlie had decided that Mateo was his super cool older best friend. And Pete knew that Mateo liked to think of Charlie as his sometimes-annoying-but-secretly-always-welcomed little brother. They'd even had a sleepover or two.

They had fun together, and Pete and Jada loved these group outings as much as the boys did. It was almost like they were a family.

At least, that's how Pete felt about it.

Mateo glanced over at him with the biggest grin on his face, and Pete couldn't help but smile. The kid was doing great. He'd finally finished up all of his community service hours, and having Charlie around to play with had been a good thing for him. Even Julieta said so.

Julieta.

Pete sucked in a deep breath and tried not to let his mind get stuck on his mom and what she was going through.

Jada lightly squeezed his hand.

"Hey."

Pete looked at her and smiled. But it was a halfhearted smile. He could feel it.

"You okay? You don't seem to be yourself tonight."

She tossed her luscious, dark brown hair over her shoulder and studied him.

Pete sighed.

"I'm sorry, baby."

"What's wrong?"

"I..." He paused, not knowing how to begin. "I got some bad news the other day, and I guess I'm just still trying to process it."

"Oh. What bad news? Is there a problem with the guardianship transfer?"

Pete looked over to make sure Mateo was still out of earshot. Then he looked at Jada, and held her hand a little tighter.

"No. That's actually going pretty well. But the lawyer we met with said that the family court judges normally wouldn't even consider making a switch like we're proposing without a compelling reason."

"A compelling reason?"

"Yeah. Like if *mamá* had a stroke or something."

Jada frowned. "Oh, okay. But you said it's going well."

"Yeah. It turns out that we actually have a compelling reason that I didn't know about."

"What is it?"

"*Mamá*. Her cancer is back."

Jada stared at him, open-mouthed.

"Pete, no."

"I had no clue until she told the lawyer. Of course, she says that she only found out herself a couple of days ago."

He drew in a deep breath and exhaled a long tired sigh.

"You say that like you don't believe her."

"No, I believe her. I do. I know she wouldn't deliberately keep something like that from me. I'm just so..."

He paused again, searching for the right words, and waiting for the lump in his throat to dissolve.

"I don't even know what I am. Angry. Terrified."

Jada ran her free hand over his knee.

"Probably a little of both. And that's perfectly all right, Pete. However you feel, it's okay."

She sighed loudly and looked over at the boys.

"I take it you haven't told Mateo yet?"

"No, we haven't."

"Are you going to?"

"Well, we're going to have to once she starts this new treatment plan the doctor's laid out. Apparently he told her they want to be a little more aggressive this time. They want to start with surgery. Then chemo. Radiation."

"Pete, if you need anything, please ask me."

Pete tried to smile at her. "Thanks, baby, but I don't want..."

Jada placed her fingers over his lips to stop him from talking, and Pete looked into her eyes.

"Pete, I'm a nurse. I love you. And I love Mateo and Julieta. Please, if you need anything... medical advice, or someone to take Julieta to appointments, or help with dinners when she's too weak to cook. Cleaning your house. Anything! Please, let me help you take care of your family."

The lump in his throat was back.

Stinging eyes.

Damn unmanly emotions.

He nodded and looked around the arcade. Anywhere but at the compassion in her eyes.

"Okay."

"Okay?"

"Yeah."

It was all he could manage.

Jada leaned in and kissed his lips.

Pete swatted at the lone tear that escaped with the back of his hand. Then caressed her face and kissed her again.

"I could really use your comfort tonight."

"Oh, yeah?"

He nodded again.

"Well, it just so happens that Charlie's other grandma is picking him up tonight for a sleepover at her house."

"Is that right?"

"Yep."

"Is that an invitation?"

"Definitely."

Pete grinned and kissed her.

———

Sidney scratched another item off of her pre-wedding TO DO list and felt a small sense of accomplishment. Alfred Hitchcock's reservation at the local Pet Palace was confirmed. Tonight's dessert — a yummy peach dump cake — was in the crockpot, ready to be transported to Adam and Bree's place for dinner. Her honeymoon suitcases were now officially packed and waiting, even though she still had no clue where they were going.

She'd taken the liberty of buying two new bikinis that afternoon on her shopping outing with her aunt and cousins, plus a super cute nightie she couldn't resist.

Their reservations for the rehearsal dinner tomorrow night had been made by Isaac's parents, Brock and Audrey Taylor —

who had also insisted on picking up the tab for that event — but Audrey had called a little while ago to let Sidney know that everything was set. They would be dining at the Jade Dragon, one of the swankiest restaurants in Cleveland, and also one of her and Ike's favorite places for gourmet Chinese cuisine. That Brock and Audrey wanted to do something special for them had meant a great deal to Isaac, though he hadn't said it in so many words.

But Sidney could tell.

It was the look in his eyes when he talked about it.

The whisper of shock, the hint of awe.

Ike and his dad still didn't have the greatest of relationships. Even though there had been a significant thaw in the last few months, Isaac still avoided spending much time in Brock's presence. And whenever they did happen to cross paths, Brock still let the occasional disparaging remark slip out.

Old habits fight death like monsters.

But Sidney was hopeful that their wedding would be a peaceful, loving, family-healing situation that would bring all of them together in cheesy-family-sitcom harmony.

She giggled to herself and pictured Ike and Brock as Greg and Mike Brady. Simon and Carlton as Theo and Cliff Huxtable.

Okay, so that last one was a stretch.

But she was still laughing when her cellphone rang.

"Hello?"

"Hello! Is this Sidney Fairchild?"

The voice was female and slightly distressed.

"It is. Who is this?"

"Ms. Fairchild, this is Lucy Morrow from Cakes a Million. I'm so sorry."

Sidney's stomach filled with rocks.

"Sorry for what?"

"We had a pipe burst last night at the bakery, and everything is ruined."

Lucy's voice was full of despair, and Sidney knew that the

woman was still talking, explaining about the extensive water damage and so forth, but she couldn't comprehend any of it.

Eyes closed, she shook her head.

"No, no, no, no, no. *No!*"

Lucy stopped talking.

"Ms. Morrow, are you telling me that my wedding cake drowned?"

"No, ma'am. I'm telling you that the bakery is completely flooded. So the good news is that we hadn't actually started making your wedding cake yet. We were scheduled to begin tomorrow."

"Okay."

"But the bad news is that now we can't make your wedding cake because the bakery is completely flooded."

Speechless.

Dumbfounded.

What?

Tears sprang immediately to her eyes, and Sidney sighed.

"I see."

It was all she could push out.

"We have a couple of names of other area bakeries that could possibly squeeze you in on such short notice. Although you most likely won't have time to do a taste testing, and they might not be able to make the flavors you wanted. But I'm happy to text the names and numbers to you."

"Sure. Thanks."

Her tone was as flat as her expectations.

"And, of course, I'll refund your deposit immediately."

"Okay."

"Again, I am so sor..."

Sidney ended the call. She just couldn't stand to listen to another apology.

"*Meow.*"

Alfred Hitchcock leapt from the back of the couch and went

trotting to the front door.

"Hey, Mr. Hitchcock, how was your day?"

Sidney held on for as long as she could, but she burst into tears just as Ike carried the cat back into the room.

"Sidney! What's wrong?"

He sounded alarmed. And now, so was she.

"What is it, Sid?"

"Our wedding is *cursed!*"

Her body rocked with sobs.

The next thing she knew, Isaac had swooped her up into his arms and carried her over to the sectional. He sat and cradled her in his arms, wiping her tears and cooing softly.

"It's all right, Sidney. Whatever it is, I promise, it'll all be okay. Everything will be okay."

He spoke as though he were trying to soothe a small child, and the tenderness of his tone only made her cry harder.

"Talk to me, darlin'. Come on now. Tell me what happened."

Sidney gulped down a breath and tried to stop the sobs.

"First my dress gets shipped around the globe, and now we don't have a wedding cake because the bakery is flooded. And the man who donated sperm so that I could be born shows up uninvited and announces he wants to get to know me because he's dying!"

Her words were stilted by sobs, like a hysterical four-year-old.

Isaac fished a lime green bandana-style handkerchief from his pocket and put it into her hands.

Sidney fiddled with it while her tears and her emotions kept flowing like a river.

"I have a substitute dress that I hate, and no wedding cake; a dying stranger wanting to be my long lost daddy; and we should've just said to hell with it and gone to Vegas like you wanted!"

She buried her face in the handkerchief, sobbing openly now, and Isaac rubbed a hand over her back in soothing circles.

"Whoa, whoa. Hold on now. Slow down. Take a deep breath for me, darlin', okay?"

Sidney took a shuddering breath and then blew her nose.

"One more time."

She took another breath, but the sobs kept wracking her body.

"Now let me get this straight... Carlton is dying?"

Sidney nodded, but she couldn't answer.

"Dying of what?"

"Tumor. It's on his spine or brain stem or something. It could be three months, or it could be three weeks, and I don't know how I'm supposed to feel about any of it."

"Oh, wow." Isaac looked troubled. "Well, you should feel however you want to feel about it, Sid. I mean, there isn't any one right way. This is a blow to you, even though you don't know him very well. Hell, just his showing up here has been a big blow. So you feel however you want to about it."

Sidney nodded, wiping tears and snot.

"I have to say... this fits with what I felt when I first met him."

"What? What did you feel?"

She knew that Ike's superpowers were strong. If he'd felt something it was probably dead on.

"Just that Carlton was broken somehow. Broken and desperate. Sad. It sort of makes sense now."

"I guess," she mumbled.

"Does Simon know any of this?"

Sidney shook her head. "Simon's been so hostile toward him, he hasn't had a chance to tell him yet."

Isaac sighed. Then he stroked a hand over her hair.

"Well, you don't worry about that, okay? That's between the two of them to figure out. Now... about the flooded bakery?"

Sidney wiped fresh tears.

"The whole place is flooded. Burst pipe and water damage.

The girl was very nice, very apologetic. We'll get our deposit back, blah, blah, blah. We still have no wedding cake!"

Her voice was a sorrowful wail, and she slumped against Ike and buried her face in the crook of his neck. Leather and citrus, a hint of sage. The masculine scent of him engulfed her senses, and when he tightened his arms around her she was finally able to take a deep, cleansing breath.

He held her that way in silence for a good five minutes.

"We should've gone to Vegas."

Her voice was calmer now. Forlorn. But calm.

"We could be married by now with none of these headaches. Especially since this isn't even my first wedding."

Her tears were silent now, but they kept coming, and she twisted Ike's handkerchief in her fingers.

"I just wanted a little bit of special for our big day. I just wanted sunshine and the water. Beautiful flowers. I wanted everything to be perfect."

Still rubbing her back, Isaac sighed.

"Aww, darlin', don't you see? It's still perfect, Sidney. We've checked the weather a million times. The sunshine will be there. So will the lake. And even if the florist shop goes up in flames tomorrow morning, the beach still has that beautiful rose garden you love, and they will still be blooming come Saturday. So the flowers will be there too. And if you and I show up, the day will be more than perfect."

He wiped her damp cheeks with his thumbs.

"You can wear a simple sundress, and we'll serve our guests cupcakes or donuts. It would still be a perfect day for me as long as we are husband and wife at the end of it."

Sidney lifted her gaze and looked into his eyes and caressed his face.

"You say the sweetest most romantic things."

Isaac grinned at her.

"Nonsense. I'm just telling it like it is. Blue skies, Sid. Nothing but blue skies and starry nights once we're man and wife."

Blue skies and starry nights.

It was their new favorite saying. Their promise to each other.

She stared at him for the longest time, just studying his handsome face. Slowly, she traced the lines of his cheekbones and his jaw with her fingers.

"Isaac?"

"Hmm?"

"Will you marry me in three days?"

He gave her that double-dimple-million-dollar-hollywood-heartthrob smile that always turned her belly into jelly.

"Now, how did you put it the second time I proposed? Oh, yeah, I remember. I will marry the crap out of you, darlin'."

Sidney giggled and dried the last of her tears, and Isaac planted a sweet kiss on her lips.

"You still feel up to having dinner with Adam and Bree and Grandad tonight?"

Sidney leaned into him.

"I could probably use the pick me up. And it'll be nice to see Sterling. Besides... maybe Bree knows a good baker who owes her a favor and can take us on extremely short notice."

Isaac kissed her again, this time slow and purposeful, making her slightly lightheaded.

His hand slithered beneath her shirt to touch her skin.

"What are you doing?"

"Well, I was hoping for a quick romp in the shower before we go."

"No. I don't think we have time for that. And I've already taken a shower."

Isaac stood, lifting her easily in his arms, and headed back to the bedroom.

"Oh, now see... we always have time for that."

15

"I'm telling you, babe," Adam Taylor swallowed down a mouthful and looked at Bree, "you really saved the day last night. The look on Sidney's face when you got off the phone with your baker friend. I mean, I thought she was going to cry."

"She did cry." Bree sighed and finished her scrambled eggs. "When we were here in the kitchen alone after dinner last night. I felt so bad for her. First the wedding gown fiasco, and now this? And her deadbeat father showing up isn't helping one bit."

"Yeah, that's a crazy situation. Ike says he told her he's dying."

"Yeah, that's what Sidney said. And I don't think it's fair of him to just show up and put that on her. He has to know what kind of stress she's already under."

"Yeah, but babe, if it's true, then he's only got a very short amount of time."

"I know." Bree shook her head. "It's a sad situation all the way around."

"Anyway, I'm just happy you were able to put a smile on her face."

Bree took a sip of her herbal tea.

"Oh, me too! And Liz sounded happy to help. She is without a doubt the best cake baker I know, and I worked plenty of weddings with her back in my catering days, so I know she'll do a great job. And that's exactly what I told Sid last night."

She took another sip and waited for Adam to respond. But when he didn't, she looked up at him, and was taken aback by the emotion on his face.

She reached out and placed her hand over his.

"Aww, babe. You're drowning in your feelings over there, aren't you?"

Adam looked at her with glistening light blue eyes, and Bree was so touched she almost welled up herself. It was rare to see her big strong husband cry.

"I just..."

He paused and shook his head, but Bree suspected he needed a minute to compose himself.

"I just can't believe that Ike is actually getting married. I mean, for so long I never thought he'd ever find peace within himself, you know? But now, he has that, and he has the love of a good woman who accepts him — weird abilities, touch issues, all of it. And I'm just so happy for him, Bree."

"I know you are."

"I'm so happy that he's going to get to have what we have, you know?"

"I know."

Adam had spent most of his life being his strange little brother's protector. His best friend and confidant. They were extremely close, and Bree loved how fiercely Adam loved him.

"I watched him struggle all of his life. And now..."

Adam pressed his fist to his lips when his voice cracked.

Bree ran her hand over his arm and then over his wavy, blond hair.

"I know, babe. I know. It's a beautiful thing. And Sidney is so perfect for him."

Adam nodded, still trying to get himself together.

The baby monitor crackled to life and baby Isla stirred. Bree looked to the living room where the little bassinet sat. But before she could move to get up from the table, Sterling Taylor walked in cradling the baby in his arms and smiling down at her. He did a slow turn in a circle as though he and his great-granddaughter were dancing.

Adam and Bree both smiled.

"Grandad, do you want me to take her?"

"Oh, no, no. A dear little innocent thing like her? She doesn't cause her great-grandaddy any discomfort at all, do you sweet pea?"

Sterling looked up at Adam then.

"I always loved babies because they never cause me pain when they touch my skin." He looked back down at baby Isla. "I imagine her Uncle Isaac will feel the same. And that will be a blessing when he starts having little ones of his own."

Bree's eyebrows shot up and she glanced over at Adam. She could tell he was just as surprised by his grandfather's words as she was.

"Can you imagine Ike with a baby?" Adam asked.

"Yes, I can. I felt so bad when Sidney had that miscarriage."

"Yeah, me too. Ike was broken up about it. Even though he tried to play the tough one for her. But I could tell."

Humming, and still slow dancing Isla around the kitchen, Sterling stared at her in wonder and addressed Adam.

"They'll get their turn soon enough. Won't they Isla? They'll give you some little cousins to play with, won't they? Yes, they will."

"Is that a psychic premonition, Grandad?"

"Oh, just something I may have seen in a vision or two."

Adam looked at Bree and made a surprised happy face, and Bree couldn't help but laugh at him. It was great to hear though. She didn't know much about Sterling, seeing as this was only his second visit to Cleveland since reuniting with his family. But if his abilities were anything like Isaac's — and she'd been told they were — then his visions would be very accurate.

"Well, I'm afraid I have to get going."

Adam wiped his mouth and stood.

"My patients aren't going to treat themselves. What's on the agenda here today?"

Bree took a deep breath and sat back in her chair.

"Well, since Sidney's been under so much stress these last few days, I'm going to use my matron of honor powers and try to get us booked for a relaxing spa day tomorrow before all the party madness begins."

"Not a bad idea."

"Right? I figure if nothing else she needs a full body massage, stat."

"As a medical professional, I couldn't agree more. If you can squeeze that in I think she'd really benefit from it."

"Agreed. Thank you for the consult, doctor."

She smiled at him and he leaned down to kiss her.

"What about you, Grandad? Got any plans before the rehearsal dinner tonight?"

"Well, as a matter of fact, I do. I've got an important conference today with Isla. We're going to get to know each other, and we're going to have a long talk about all the proud psychics in her family."

"Okay then."

Adam kissed his fingers and then placed them on Isla's forehead, and Bree recognized it as the safest way he could give his little girl a kiss without accidentally touching his Grandfather.

When Adam had left the room, Bree looked at Sterling.

"So... this psychic gene in your family?"

"Yes?"

"Does it always follow a direct line from parent to child, or is there any chance that Isla might develop these powers?"

———

"Still nothing from the divers?"

Isaac rocked back in his desk chair and looked up at Gavin.

"Nope. They've been at it for close to 24 hours now, and I understand that the Coast Guard has offered their support. How much longer you want to give them?"

"I'm going to let this be your call, Sergeant. What are you thinking?"

Isaac blew air through his lips and tapped the top of his desk with the eraser end of the pencil in his hands and thought about the body count.

"Seven dead, nine wounded, one still likely. Finding the gun is a long shot, especially with the way that river was rushing yesterday. But with a body count like that I say we give them a little more time."

Gavin nodded.

"How about we give them 'til the 36 hour mark then call them off?"

"Agreed. You'll have the paperwork on your desk before shift change."

"And the other matter?"

Isaac glanced over at Pete, who was watching and listening intently, before he turned back to Gavin.

"Hiroshi confirmed that the vic was poisoned." Isaac pulled a print out from his desk and handed it to Gavin. "Toxicology report from the independent lab indicates lethal levels of oleandrin and neriine, both of which are found in every part of the oleander plant. It's a shrub that's used in…"

"My grandmother had an oleander hedge down in Savannah, Georgia. It was beautiful. But she would always warn us kids not to touch it with bare hands because the sap could irritate the skin."

"Well, apparently Gregory Townsend was poisoned with it.

Pete and I would like to let this one simmer until after I get back from my honeymoon. The up side here is that our pool of suspects has no clue that we've been able to determine a cause of death. We're hoping that maybe one of them will trip up in the next two weeks and give us a person of interest."

Gavin nodded. "Sounds good."

"Thank you. That means when I leave out of here tonight, I can concentrate on getting hitched."

"Yeah, and for the next two weeks, I'll be attached to Runyan and Spencer, helping with their cases."

Pete's tone indicated he wasn't exactly thrilled about being the third wheel to the two newest hires.

"Think of it this way, Pete." Isaac grinned at him. "You're not the rookie detective in homicide anymore."

Pete pointed a finger at him.

"That's true. Spencer's the rookie detective now."

"And you can give him a hard time, and catch them both up on all the department gossip while I'm gone."

"Just don't mention anything about me," Gavin said.

"Or me," Isaac added.

"Well, without you two, there is no gossip! Don't tie my hands like that."

Gavin and Isaac laughed at him, and then Gavin headed back to his office.

As soon as he walked away, Isaac's cellphone rang. He looked at the screen and frowned. Not because he didn't want to speak to the person calling. It was just that the person had never called him before.

"Oliver?"

Isaac heard the trepidation in his own voice, but it couldn't be helped. His younger brother never called him.

Ever.

"Hey, Ike. You got a sec?"

"Sure. Everything okay?"

"Yeah. Why wouldn't it be?"

"Oh, I don't know. Maybe because you've never called me before."

"Sure I have."

"No, Oli, you haven't. What's up? You're not downstairs in the jail, are you?"

He was only half joking with that question. After all, just a few months ago, Oliver had been a person of interest in a murder.

"Very funny! No, I'm not in jail. Listen I just have a question for you about your wedding."

"Okay, what about it?"

"Well, Emily's bringing a date. Did you know that?"

"Yeah, I know it. So?"

"Well, can I bring a date too?"

He sounded like a five-year-old tattling on his twin sister.

"I want a lollipop too!"

"Yes, you have a plus one, Oli. It said so on the invitation."

"Oh, it did?"

"Yes."

"So, you don't need to like, alert the caterers or anything?"

Isaac sighed.

"No. We've already allotted for a few extra mouths in the catering budget for surprise guests at the reception. Thank you for checking, but you are free to bring a plus one."

"Okay, cool. Now, do the dates come with us tonight at the rehearsal dinner too?"

"Uh, well since Mom and Dad are footing the bill for tonight, I think that's a question for them."

"Shit. All right then. Thanks."

The line went dead before Isaac could respond.

"Goodbye to you too," he mumbled and set his cellphone aside.

"That sounded like an interesting conversation."

Pete was clearly trying not to laugh.

"Yeah, well, you know Oliver."

"Your younger brother does seem to be a character. You know, I've met all three of your siblings, and he is definitely..."

"Different?"

"Yes. Good word. He's definitely different."

"Shady's a better word. Not exactly a criminal, but not truly upstanding either. Hard to believe we're related, right?"

"Hey. Me and my sister are the same way, you know that. I'm a cop. She's a felon." Pete shrugged a shoulder. "Families, man."

Isaac nodded.

"Yeah. Families."

Pete looked at him and grinned.

"So, you getting cold feet?"

"Nope."

"Not even a little, huh?"

"Nope. I can't wait."

"Jada says that Sidney's kind of having a tough time of it."

Isaac sighed.

"Yeah. She's had a string of bad luck with her wedding dress and now the cake. But we'll get through it. 'Cause the dress and the cake... that's all just window dressing, you know? The important thing is that we'll be married by the end of the day on Saturday, and it doesn't matter what we wear or eat."

"It matters to her though."

Isaac sighed again, this time deeper, and his shoulders sagged.

"Yeah, I know. Bree found us a terrific baker who agreed to take over the wedding cake duties, so that's settled. But there's nothing anyone can do about the lost dress. It was one of a kind. The dress maker found her one from that same collection that's close to the original, and everybody seems to think is perfect, but Sid's not so sure about it. And I don't know how to fix that."

"I don't think you can."

"No. Me either."

Isaac couldn't hide the sorrow in his own voice. He just

wanted to make things perfect for Sidney, but he knew he was powerless.

"Jada says you're writing your own vows?"

"Yeah. Sid really wanted to, so..."

He let the end of that sentence dangle.

"And?"

"And what?"

"And, have you written yours yet?"

Isaac hesitated.

"Well, I've still got some time."

"Mmm. Jada says Sidney's written hers already."

"Boy, Jada's keeping close tabs on my wedding plans, isn't she?" Pete laughed.

"You know how women are. She and Sid are close. They've spent hours talking about your wedding."

"Yeah, I know."

"Well, you better get to writing."

"Yeah, and you better be careful. Sounds like Jada might be gathering wedding tips for herself."

Pete laughed, but Isaac just stared at him.

"No. Trust me. Marriage is the last thing on my girl's mind." Pete sounded confident. "We're just now settling into a really good place, you know. We took it slow, got to know each other. Got the boys together. We're in a good groove now."

"Uh huh. Still just so-called friends?"

"No."

"No?"

"No, we finally danced back over that line about a month ago. It's tricky with Charlie always around, but occasionally we get an evening to ourselves."

"No wedding bells though?"

Pete laughed. "Let's just get you hitched first, okay?"

"All right."

They each turned to their computers, but Isaac couldn't

concentrate on anything except what to write for his wedding vows.

———

Sidney's leg bounced up and down and she stared out the window at the passing scenery. She jumped slightly when Isaac reached over and took her hand.

"Darlin' you are wound tighter than a stressed out cuckoo clock. What's going on? Why are you so nervous tonight?"

She sighed and placed her free hand on top of his, giving it a light squeeze.

"I don't know, I just..."

She paused and shook her head.

"Sidney." He glanced at her before his gaze went back to the road. "Talk to me. Baby, if this wedding is stressing you out this much, I say let's toss all the plans into the lake and go to the courthouse and get married. Just be done with it."

"You don't mean that."

"I do mean that."

He pulled the car into the parking lot of Lakeview Park Beach and quickly found a spot. Then he turned his whole body to face her and took both her hands in his.

"Sidney, look at me."

Sidney leaned into the seat and stared into his gorgeous grey eyes. Normally light in color and crystal clear, she watched them darken in intensity as he studied her.

"This should be the happiest time of our lives right now, but instead it's been full of family turmoil and one crisis after another. And I know that weddings are always stressful, but I just hate seeing you like this."

"I'm sorry. I don't mean to be so anxious. But I'd be lying if I said I wasn't expecting some fireworks tonight. Simon is not happy that I've allowed Carlton to stay, and he doesn't understand why I invited him to the rehearsal dinner with the rest of us."

"He doesn't have to understand it."

Isaac's tone was simple and straightforward.

"Hell, I don't have to understand it. It's your wedding and he's your father. If you want him here, then Simon has no right to try and persuade you otherwise."

"I know. But the thing is, Ike... I'm not even sure why I've let Carlton stay myself. Maybe I let his diagnosis get to me."

"Maybe you did."

Still holding her hands, Isaac spread them apart in a "so what" gesture.

"You're allowed to take pity on a dying man, Sidney. Especially when that dying man is your father. Even though he is a perfect stranger to you. That's the very definition of compassion, darlin'. And you have it in spades. It's one of the reasons I love you so much."

Sidney reached up and caressed his much too handsome face, letting the tip of her thumb trace over his dimple. God, how did she get so lucky to find him?

"I love you back, baby. More than you will ever know."

He brought her hand to his lips and kissed the palm of it. Then he leaned in and kissed her, soft at first. Sweet and innocent. Then more insistent, his tongue probing, tangling with hers.

They were both breathless when they finally pulled away, and he rested his forehead on hers.

"Do you think anyone would notice if we turned around and went home? Let them do the rehearsal and the dinner without us, and we go home and make love?"

"Hmm." Sidney glanced around as though she were actually considering it. "I like your plan. But I think they'd notice."

"Really?"

"Well, we are kind of the stars of the show."

"Damn. You're probably right."

She took in a deep breath. "I'm really worried about Carlton saying something insensitive and offending... well, everyone."

"That's okay. I'm sure my dad will say something insensitive at some point too. He can't help himself. Except he'll probably only offend me and Grandad."

He gave her a look, and Sidney couldn't help but laugh.

He grinned at her.

"Come on. Let's go practice getting married."

An event coordinator from the Sunset Terrace restaurant met them in their designated section of the beach, where workers were busy making sure the sand and the surrounding areas were pristine for the coming nuptials. The section they'd rented was roped off with signs saying they were preparing for a wedding that weekend.

Sidney had rented a driftwood arch from the florist that was being installed, and on the big day it would be covered in her chosen flowers. Standing there now, Sidney could almost picture it. It was going to be beautiful.

Their families slowly began to trickle in from the parking lot, and they were joined by the pastor of a nearby church who would be performing the ceremony on Saturday.

Much to Sidney's delight, the mood of the gathering was light and airy, mimicking the early evening, and covered by the peachy glow of the setting sun. The waves lapped at the sand, and the gulls called out overhead as handshakes and hugs were exchanged, and everyone gave the wedding coordinator and the officiant their attention.

Maybe this wouldn't be such a bad evening after all.

Her family and Isaac's appeared to be meshing well, everyone on their best behavior.

Carlton was charming.

Brock was accommodating.

Audrey and Aunt Bobbie were laughing and talking.

Sure Simon steered clear of Carlton, and Sterling steered clear of Brock. But really, both were good things as far as Sidney was concerned.

"Perfect!"

The wedding coordinator was cheerful and efficient as she worked to place Adam and Bree, and the little bell-ringer, where they would stand for the actual ceremony.

"Now for the bride, and the father of the bride," she called out. "Meet me at the top of the aisle, please."

"That's my cue." Sidney winked at Isaac and headed over to where the coordinator waited.

She saw the collision coming.

A speeding train heading straight for the giant immovable object.

Inside her, the impact of the crash detonated.

Simon and Carlton came face-to-face right in front of her.

"You lost?"

Simon's tone dripped icicles.

Carlton's big genuine smile dropped like a stone.

"No. I'm sorry. I wasn't thinking. She called for the father of the bride and I moved. It was instinct, that's all."

"Instinct?" Simon's smile was vicious. "Oh, like you ever had a fatherly instinct in your life. Man, get outta my face with that shit."

Carlton looked deflated.

"Simon, if you could just..."

"I said get out of my face!"

"Stop it!"

Sidney screamed at them, her voice carrying all over the beach.

All chatter stopped.

All eyes zeroed in on her.

Even the gulls went silent.

She didn't care. She'd had it.

"I can't take this anymore. I'm getting married in two days and nothing is going right this week. And I can't take this constant bickering between the two of you! Now I don't want to do this, but I will find someone else to walk me down the aisle if I have to."

"Sidney calm..."

"Sterling?"

Sidney ignored Simon's words, pushed past him, and marched over to where Isaac stood with his grandfather. Sterling turned toward her with mild concern on his gentle face.

"What is it, my dear?"

She wiped a wayward tear from her cheek and looked at him.

"I know this is a big ask, but would you..."

She paused and glanced back over her shoulder at her brother and Carlton before she addressed Sterling again.

"Would you be willing to walk me down the aisle?"

Sterling's smile was so full of love it nearly made her fall into his arms.

"Why, I would be delighted and honored."

She smiled at him, and both Simon and Carlton made their way over to her.

"All right, you've made your point, Sid."

Simon sounded contrite.

"I wasn't trying to make a point. I was making a decision."

"I'm sorry, all right? I truly am." Simon looked her in the eyes. "Come on. I will play nice with Carlton, okay? I promise."

"Yeah, and I'll back off," Carlton added. "From here on out I am just a wedding guest. I'll sit back and stay out of Simon's way. I'm just happy to be here."

Carlton leaned in and kissed Sidney's cheek, and then he walked a few yards away to a bench in the grass and sat down.

Sidney turned back to Sterling.

"Sterling... I..."

Sterling patted her hand with his white cotton-gloved one and smiled as he cut her off.

"No problem, my dear. I'm always happy to help."

Sidney smiled at him.

"Imagine that I kissed your cheek, okay?"

Sterling placed his gloved hand on his cheek and made a giddy face.

Sidney laughed and then turned her attention back to Simon. She gave her brother a good long withering stare.

"I'm sorry, sis. Making trouble at your wedding is the very last thing I ever wanted to do."

"I know."

"It's just that man. I know I shouldn't let him, but he gets under my skin, Sid. The way he waltzed in here like he belonged. I just can't stand it. He's so full of himself. He's..."

"He's dying, Simon."

Simon stopped talking and stared at her.

"What?"

"Carlton. He's dying. He left the hospital against his doctor's advice. They don't give him long. Three months, if that."

A small burst of laughter sprang from Simon's lips. Then he stopped and stared at her again, all traces of humor gone.

"Did he tell you that? And you fell for it? That's how he wormed his way into the middle of your wedding?"

"Simon."

Sidney put her hands on her hips, and she could tell the tone of her voice had her big brother backing up. His lips clamped into a tight thin line and he glanced off at the water.

"Talk to him. Have a conversation with him, Simon. Set the hostility aside, and just have a civil conversation with the man. Do it for me."

"No." He pointed a finger at her. "Don't you do that. Don't ask me to do it for you."

"Too late. I already did. No take backs, remember."

Simon let out a heavy sigh.

"I'll think about it."

"I'd do it for you."

"Oh, Sidney."

It was a how-could-you-pour-on-the-guilt type of groan, and Sidney knew she had him.

"Well, I would. And you know it."

"Yes. I do."

Growing up, they'd always made each other a high priority. There was nothing she wouldn't do for her brother. And she knew he would do anything for her.

"Fine. Before the weekend is over, I will talk to him."

"Thank you. Now can we please stop wasting the event coordinator's time and rehearse getting me hitched?"

He grinned and gave her his arm, and they walked back over to the top of the aisle.

————

When rehearsal was over, they all piled back into their cars and drove back into the city to the Jade Dragon Chinese restaurant.

On the drive over, Isaac reached over and took Sidney by the hand.

"For a minute there, I thought I was going to have to ask your brother and your father to leave."

He glanced over at her and she grinned.

"I thought the way you handled the situation was perfect though."

"You did?"

"I did. You stood up for yourself and managed to put them in their places without putting either one of them down. And you made my grandad happy at the same time."

She giggled and Isaac brought her hand up and kissed it.

"I hope he wasn't disappointed when I rescinded the offer."

"Not at all. He knew the role you wanted him to play. And I think he was happy to do it."

"Well, I certainly appreciated it. And it made Simon very apologetic, so..."

She let the rest of that sentence dangle.

"It seemed to back Carlton off too."

"Yeah."

"In fact, I think it put him on his very best behavior. There wasn't another peep out of him the rest of the rehearsal."

"No. Honestly, I think he went and sat on that bench because he wasn't feeling well."

"Oh. How could you tell?"

"When he came by the house the other morning... you know, when he told me he was dying?"

"Yeah?"

"Well, at one point we were sitting at the table talking, and he was eating his waffle. He dropped his fork. And it wasn't like a regular slip of the hand either. It was more like... well, like he couldn't feel his hand. Like it just went numb or something. He held both his arms kind of... stiff. It was like he couldn't move them, not even if he'd tried."

"Wow."

"Tonight when he went to sit on that bench, I thought I saw him holding his arms like that again. I think he must be experiencing some kind of intermittent paralysis." She rolled her eyes. "But I'm no doctor. I mean, what do I know?"

"That sounds awful."

"Yeah."

"I take it Simon still doesn't know what's going on?"

"I told him."

"You did?"

"Yeah. I felt I had to."

"How'd he take it?"

"He didn't believe it at first. Actually, I'm still not sure he believes me. But I asked him to have a civil conversation with Carlton."

"Think he'll do it?"

"He promised he would."

"Well, hopefully they can come to some kind of cease fire for the weekend. For their sakes."

"For their sakes?"

"Yes. Because if they keep upsetting you, I'm going to have to hurt one or both of them, and I really don't want to have do that. I like Simon; I would hate to ruin the friendship we've been building. And Carlton is dying, so that would just be wrong."

When they got to the restaurant, he turned off the car and looked at her.

"So, I guess after tonight, we're not supposed to see each other all day tomorrow?"

"Well, we'll see each other in the morning, obviously. But then yeah, we'll be apart the rest of the time until the wedding. Bree has us booked at some day spa place tomorrow morning before the bachelor and bachelorette parties. And I think Erika is going to spend the night at the house with me tomorrow night."

Isaac grunted. Why he couldn't stay in his own house with the woman he loved the night before their wedding, he'd never understand.

"What about you? What's on your agenda for tomorrow?"

"Oh, Adam's booked us at the spa for facials and pedicures too."

"What?"

She grinned at his joke.

"Yeah, I thought maybe I'd get a perm for the wedding."

"Don't you dare!"

Sidney laughed out loud, and Isaac smiled. He loved putting a smile on her pretty face, especially since she'd been so stressed out the past few days.

"Come on."

They got out of the car and he led her inside the restaurant, where they had the private room reserved for their party.

The room was decked out with the finest Chinese wedding decor Isaac had ever seen. There were a thousand red paper lanterns hanging from the ceiling, and ornate centerpieces featuring red candles and flowers on the long wood table. The wall beyond the table was covered in red paper flowers of various sizes with *Isaac and Sidney* spelled out in gold letters. It was stunning.

"Oh, my gosh!"

Sidney sounded as astonished as Isaac felt. She left his side and rushed to his mother, Audrey.

"It's beautiful, Audrey! You guys didn't have to do all of this."

Sidney hugged both of his parents, and Isaac awkwardly gave his mom a hug, being careful not to touch any exposed skin.

"Thanks, Mom. You went all out."

"Oh, nothing is too good for my son and his bride. Besides, it was so much fun to plan, and I think the owner of the restaurant got a kick out of it too."

"How in the world did you get them to do this, Mom?"

"Simple. I asked nicely."

Isaac laughed at the matter-of-fact tone of her voice. She was clearly very pleased with herself, and he loved it.

"Well, you outdid yourself. This is amazing, and Sid and I really appreciate it. Thank you."

"You're welcome!"

Audrey moved carefully and gave him another hug, and Isaac tried his hardest not to tense up as he hugged her back.

"Uh... she had a little help, you know?"

The sly comment came from his father, and Isaac turned to his dad with an anxious smile.

"Okay, so this was all Audrey's idea, and her vision. But she couldn't have done it without my credit card."

"Thank you, Dad." Isaac bowed slightly in his direction. "Sidney and I are blown away."

"Yes, we are!" Sidney echoed from a few feet away, where she stood examining the elaborate centerpieces with Bree and Erika.

Isaac chuckled and turned back to his dad.

"This is so great. Thank you."

A satisfied grin worked it's way over Brock's face, and Isaac couldn't help but wonder if the satisfaction was because he was pleased they liked it, or because he was pleased Isaac had to thank him.

"You're welcome. It was our pleasure to do it."

They stared at each other for a moment longer.

"She is a lovely girl, Isaac. Your mother and I are both quite taken with her. We're... *I'm*... I-I'm very happy for you."

Isaac's insides turned gooey.

Was his father expressing... sentiment?

A fond emotion?

For *him?*

Isaac swallowed past the sudden and unmanly lump in his throat and looked his father in the eyes.

"Thank you, Dad. That means a lot to me."

Brock took a deep breath and then slowly reached out and placed a steady hand on Isaac's shoulder.

Isaac's breath stilled.

Brock's hand tightened. Then he gave a curt nod.

When Brock let go and stepped away without another word, Isaac let go of his held breath.

The stiffness of his chest melted.

"That was my son's equivalent of a hug." Sterling sounded impressed. "I think he was actually trying to be mindful of your touch issues for once."

Isaac took a cleansing breath and looked at his grandfather.

"Yeah. I think you're right."

"Weddings are wondrous things." Sterling grinned at him.

"That they are, Grandad. That they are."

Everyone sat down to the delicious Chinese feast then, and

Isaac glanced around the table and smiled at all the different conversations going on. Their families appeared to be getting along like old friends.

His mom and Sidney's Aunt Bobbie were engaged in a lively discussion about weddings — each of theirs and their children's. His dad, Uncle Frank and Simon were having an animated debate about sports. Bree and Sidney were busy being charmed by one of Sterling's many stories. Sid's cousin Tameka and her husband, Jamal, were talking among themselves and taking care of their little boy. Emily and Erika were laughing at something Oliver said, while Adam and Carlton seemed to be embroiled in a frank discussion about race in America.

And that was the one conversation that grabbed Isaac's attention.

He watched them closely, listening intently to what they were saying. The discourse covered such ground as police brutality, the N word being used in rap songs, and Adam's uncertainty about repeating that word in the rap songs he loved so much. But what struck Isaac the most was that both men displayed an inherent sense of respect throughout the entire conversation.

Voices were never raised.

Tempers never flared.

They spoke openly and honestly about the subject and nobody's feelings got bruised.

Sidney leaned into Isaac's side and Isaac smiled and wrapped an arm around her.

"This is nice."

"Yes, it is." He leaned in and kissed her lips. Seeing her this relaxed made him immensely happy.

The clink of a spoon on glass got their attention, and he turned to see Adam now standing and commanding attention.

"I'm sorry to interrupt your dinner and your conversations, but I just wanted us all to take a moment and raise a glass. Not to the happy couple... I'll get to that toast at the reception on Saturday. Tonight, I just want to toast to my future sister-in-law."

A soft murmur of *'aww'* went around the table, and Isaac looked to his side to see Sidney wide-eyed with surprise.

"Sidney, I know that I don't have to tell you that none of us Taylors ever thought that we'd get here. Not even Ike."

Isaac chuckled and looked at Sidney. "True story."

"But you waltzed in and changed everything," Adam continued. "You changed *everything*. Now, my brother is happier than he's ever been. He's calmer. More sure of himself. More comfortable in his own skin. And that's all because of you."

Adam paused, and to Isaac's utter surprise, his big brother teared up.

Isaac's stomach tightened.

He blinked rapidly when his own eyes suddenly burned with tears.

Adam looked down for a few seconds to get his emotions under control, and Isaac swallowed hard.

"And we are grateful," Adam finally finished with glistening eyes. "Welcome to the family, doll."

An echo of 'welcome to the family' went around the table, and Sidney wiped tears from her cheeks.

"Thank you," she said softly.

When Adam sat down, Simon stood.

"Well, Adam may not want to toast the groom, but I definitely do."

"Uh oh," Isaac said, sniffing and trying to lighten the mood.

Simon and everyone else laughed.

"It'll be manly, I promise." Simon deepened his voice and grinned.

Isaac laughed.

"I, uh... I don't think any of you can know what it was like for me, being half a world away in Japan and knowing that my baby sister, my partner in crime, was in real trouble and on her own."

Simon paused and sighed. "In a word, it was torture. I was terrified for her safety. Little did I know that she had someone here to watch over her and keep her safe. You were there for Sidney when I couldn't be, Ike. And you saved her life on more than one occasion. For that, I am eternally grateful to you. I know that you will continue to look after her in the years to come. And I'm looking forward to finally having a brother who loves basketball as much as I do!"

Everyone laughed, and Simon raised his glass.

"Welcome to the family, my brother."

"Welcome to the family, Isaac!" Bobbie called out.

The sentiment was echoed around the table.

Isaac smiled and nodded at them.

"Thank you all."

Food, conversation, and laughter continued after the impromptu toasts, and at one point Sidney pulled out her cellphone and began snapping pictures of everyone.

"So, Grandad?" Emily spoke up. "How long will you be here? If you're not leaving right after the wedding, I'd love to spend an afternoon with you while you're here."

"Oh, no, my dear. I'll be here forever now."

Isaac frowned and looked at him, as did every other Taylor in the room.

"What do you mean, Sterling?" Bree asked.

"Well, I'm not going back to Tennessee. I've decided to move here to Cleveland, to be near Isaac and make up for lost time. I've already let my apartment at the retirement village go, and I boxed up my things and had them shipped."

Sterling turned to Adam.

"Oh, they should be arriving next Wednesday, okay?"

Adam looked dumbfounded. "Um... okay."

Isaac was shocked.

Brock looked positively livid.

"Uh... Grandad? Are you sure you want to do that?" Isaac studied his grandfather. "I mean, that's a really big decision."

"Why, yes, it is."

Sterling's slow Southern drawl was full of light and mischief.

"And it's one that's already been made. We've got a lot to catch up on, wouldn't you agree?"

Isaac imagined a spotlight springing to life over his head.

All eyes turned to him.

How the hell was he supposed to answer that question? As far as he knew, Sidney's family — with the exception of Simon — had zero clue about his crazy psychic abilities. Let alone that it was a family trait.

"Um... well, yeah, I mean, that... that would be great, Grandad, but..."

"Once again, the crazy takes center stage."

Brock's tone was biting.

"And we were all having such a good time."

Audrey placed her hand on Brock's arm, and Isaac thought he actually looked apologetic.

"Some of us are still having a good time, son."

"Why are you doing this, old man?" Brock glared at his father from across the table. "Things are just fine the way they are."

"Things are not fine. Isaac's training is woefully behind where it should be by now. Where it *would be* if we hadn't been kept apart all those years. I'm doing what's necessary for him. Thankfully, he's a grown man now and can do what he wants. He's no longer under your thumb."

"He's in a good place now, Dad. He doesn't need you bringing..."

"All right, stop!"

Isaac's well-practiced cop voice got everyone's attention.

He pointed at his dad and his grandfather.

"Both of you."

His gaze bounced back and forth between them.

"Not another word about this matter. We are here to celebrate Sid's and my wedding, and I will not let the two of you turn it into a shouting match."

The long pause was filled with the plinky-plunky restaurant music and tension so thick you could reach out and give it a squeeze.

"I'm sorry, Isaac. You're absolutely right." Sterling turned to Sidney. "Forgive me, my dear. I did not mean to sour this celebration."

Sidney smiled at him, and Isaac tried to relax.

"I apologize as well. To you both."

Brock's voice was stiff, but laced with sincerity.

The low rumble of chatter began again, like a video game resetting itself.

Isaac slumped back in his chair, and Sidney took his hand and leaned into him.

"We're going to survive our wedding. Right?" she whispered.

Isaac laced their fingers together.

"I hear people do. Somehow."

16

"This is madness, Sid."

"Isaac, please. It's been such a stressful week already. I don't want to fight with you on top of everything else."

"I don't want to fight with you either, darlin'. But I also don't want you running around at all hours of the night in your efforts to help this woman get away from her abuser either. Especially not so close to our wedding. Anything could happen."

It had been a wonderful evening of delicious food and great conversation spent with both of their families. But in the car on the way home, a simple little comment about driving Beth and Kylee to the airport had sparked a full blown argument.

An argument that had followed them all the way home.

"Isaac, you know that I have to do this. I'll be back in a couple of hours. It's just one little trip to the airport. There's no danger in that."

"Really? For all you know, the asshole she's running from could be stalking her. Didn't you tell me that he's somehow been managing to get threatening texts and notes to her?"

"Well, yes, but..."

"What if he's staking out the Hope House right now, just

waiting for a chance to grab her when she's least expecting it? What if he's somewhere watching when you pick up this woman and her daughter, and he follows you to the airport?"

"What do you want me to do, Ike?"

She hadn't meant to raise her voice, but there it was. And all the fight suddenly fled when Isaac looked as though she'd slapped him.

They stared at each other for a long silent moment.

"I'm sorry. I..." She had no clue what to say. "I have to go."

Isaac's gaze bore into her, his grey eyes dark as a storm cloud. His jaw was set, his lips were thin and twisted into a frown so crestfallen Sidney felt it in her bones.

Her stomach churned and burned. She hated being at odds with him.

She turned for the door.

"Hell of a way to end such a great night."

The bitterness of his tone bit at her back.

"Happy rehearsal dinner, darlin'."

The words jabbed at her heart like a jagged knife.

She turned back around and looked at him.

"Are you making me choose, Isaac? Between you and helping this woman?"

"No. I would never make you choose, Sid. But do you remember back when I told you that I had to go out at night and try to stop a man from committing a terrible crime? Just some random flash of the future that I'd seen when someone bumped into me. And you asked me not to go alone?"

Sidney did remember that night. Something about the look in his eyes that night had made her worry. They were so determined. So resigned. He'd caught a rapist that night, with a little help from his partner.

"I do remember."

"Well, I'm asking you not to go alone."

The parking lot appeared full, but through the wall of windows at the front of the Cleveland Hopkins International Airport, Sidney could see the ticket counters weren't very busy at all. Not surprising at this time of night, she supposed.

She glanced at the clock in her car.

11:43 pm.

"Your flight takes off in about 45 minutes. The good thing is that we've already checked you in via the app on my phone, so you should just be able to go straight to the gate."

"I hope the ID you got for me is convincing."

"My guy does good work. You shouldn't have a problem. A few parting words of advice? Stay off of social media. That is the quickest way for Hank to find you."

"No social media. Not even tempted."

"We've ditched your cellphone, just get a new one once you get where you're going."

"Right."

Sidney handed over the manilla envelope containing Beth's new papers.

"Don't forget to change your appearance. That's important. Remember to keep educating yourself about your new hometown. And once you're settled somewhere, enroll in a self-defense course or a kickboxing class or something similar. Learning to take care of yourself does wonders for your self-esteem and your confidence."

"Thank you for everything, Sidney."

"You're welcome. I'll be looking for a postcard from Bonnie and Katie Westborn in the next month or two."

"You'll get it."

They all got out of the car, and Sidney glanced around at the nearly deserted parking lot. Then she opened the back seat to pull out Beth's bag and Kylee's backpack.

"Where do you think you're going, bitch?"

The voice was a snarl, and Sidney looked up to see a big lumberjack-looking man with a full beard and a flannel shirt.

"Hank!"

The panic in Beth's voice sparked terror in Sidney's gut.

"I told you, you're not leaving me. Kylee is mine and so are you."

He grabbed Beth by the arm and jerked her to him.

"Kylee, run!"

Beth's voice was a terrified shriek.

The child obeyed her mother and took off across the parking lot.

"Kylee? You get back here right now!" Hank shouted.

Sidney took the distraction to pull her gun from her purse and level it at him.

"Let her go!"

"Shut up, bitch! This is none of your business."

"I said let her go!"

Hank yanked Beth in front of him, like a human shield.

Fear and dread hit Sidney's stomach like toxic waste.

"My wife and kid are coming with me."

"I am not your wife!"

"You and Kylee belong to me."

"I don't think they do."

Isaac stuck his gun to the back of Hank's head. His voice calm as a summer's breeze.

The shock in Hank's eyes turned to rage in an instant.

He shoved Beth forward, knocking her into Sidney, sending them both to the ground.

Then he turned on Isaac with a savage yell.

From her vantage point on the ground, Sidney saw Ike send Hank's head barreling into the open passenger side doorframe of her car with just a flick of his hand.

The blow was swift and hard.

Hank was out cold before he hit the ground.

"You all right, darlin'?"

"I'm good."

Sidney stood and helped Beth up.

"Kylee! Where's Kylee?"

"She's with my partner." Ike pointed across the parking lot.

"Mommy!"

The little girl came running with Pete following behind.

"This is the dirtbag?" Pete asked.

"Yep." Isaac handed Pete his handcuffs. "Would you mind?"

"Allow me."

Once they had Hank cuffed and stuffed into the back of Ike's car, Sidney turned to Beth.

"What are you going to do now?"

Beth looked perplexed.

"What do you mean? Kylee and I are getting on a plane."

"Sure you want to do that, ma'am?" Isaac asked.

"I'm sure I want this nightmare to end. I just want Hank out of our lives. I want my little girl to be safe from him."

"Now that we've got him in custody there's a good chance that you don't have to upend your lives in order to make that happen. And your testimony would no doubt go a long way toward putting him behind bars where he belongs."

"It's your choice, Beth. You and Kylee can get on that plane and flee. Or you can stay and help make sure Hank can never hurt either one of you ever again. And if things don't go the way you want them to, you can always use those new papers of yours at a later time."

Clutching her daughter close, Beth worried her bottom lip and looked down at the ground. Kylee looked up at her mother.

"Can we put daddy in jail for hurting us?"

"Yes, that's what they're saying, honey."

"Let's do that. Then I can go back to my school and daddy won't hit you anymore. And he won't... touch me anymore."

Tears hit Beth's cheeks.

"Okay. We'll stay and testify. But, can we still stay at the shelter? Just in case he makes bail or something?"

Sidney smiled at her.

"Yes, you can. Let's get you back there now."

When Beth and Kylee were back in her car, Sidney turned to Isaac.

"Thank you for being here and coming to my rescue."

He pulled her into his arms.

"Thank you for letting me."

"You stopped him with your superpowers. I saw it."

"Just as long as no one else saw it."

"Isaac, did you know? That something like this would happen? I mean... did you see it in a vision or something?"

"Let's just say I had a feeling."

"You said that about my dad."

"With your dad it was different. I didn't touch him. I just looked at him and... I don't know... *sensed* it? That's the best way I can describe it."

She studied him.

"So you saw something when you touched me recently. Is that it?"

"I didn't see anything. But yes, I touched you and I felt... danger."

"Why didn't you just tell me?"

"I didn't want to worry you."

"Well. Thank you for insisting on following me."

He kissed her forehead and then her lips.

"Drive safe, darlin'. I'll be home as soon as we get Hank dropped off at intake."

"Okay. Be careful."

"Always. I love you."

"I love you back."

17

*T*he next morning, Sidney and Isaac slept in. Something neither one of them got to do very often. But she woke to the wonderful smell of bacon and coffee.

That made her nervous.

She slipped out of bed and pulled on her robe. Then she ventured down the hall to the living room.

The O'Jays were singing, inviting everybody aboard the "Love Train," and Isaac was bopping around the kitchen, pouring coffee and plating up turkey bacon and toast.

"Are you cooking?"

"Hey! Good morning, beautiful. I was trying to surprise you with breakfast in bed."

"And you're *cooking!*"

A terrifying thought, to be sure.

"Not really. It's just turkey bacon, which I nuked in the microwave, toast with butter and jam and some sliced cantaloupe. Nothing I can really burn or scorch or use to set the house on fire."

Sidney looked up into his ruggedly handsome face.

"You are so adorable."

"Well, I'm glad you think so. Now go get back in bed so I can serve you."

Sidney laughed.

"No, you don't need to bring me breakfast in bed. I'm up now, let's just sit and eat."

"Oh, okay."

He sounded like she'd taken all the fun out of his surprise, but he carried the food over to the table anyway.

She watched him as they ate in silence.

"Isaac?"

"Yes?"

"I really love you."

He set his coffee down and looked into her eyes.

"I really love you too, darlin'. What do you say we prove it tomorrow? Meet me on the beach at 11:30 in the morning and marry me."

"You've got a date."

She leaned in and kissed him.

"What are you doing today while I'm at the spa with Jada and Bree?"

"Just some last minute odds and ends. I need to pack for our honeymoon. I need to drop Mr. Hitchcock off at the Pet Palace for his vacation."

"Oh, he has to be there by noon."

"I know."

"And don't forget to take his little fish that makes the crinkle noise when he attacks it. They said he could bring his favorite toy with him."

"I remember. I've already put it in the bag with his food."

"I'm going to miss him."

"He'll be fine."

"I know. But he'll be gone two whole weeks."

"So will we. And trust me, you and I are going to be so busy, we won't have time to miss our cat."

Sidney gasped and gave him her best playfully shocked face.

"How can you say that? He's our baby!"

"Well, just think. When he comes home, his parents will officially be married."

She smiled. "I like the sound of that."

"Me too."

She glanced at the clock on the wall.

"Oh, shoot. I need to get moving. Something tells me Jada and Bree are going to be prompt."

She got up and took her empty plate to the kitchen. Then she kissed Ike's lips and dashed off to the bedroom singing, "I'm getting married tomorrow!"

———

Sidney's afternoon was spent being thoroughly pampered. A body polish treatment, followed by a deep tissue massage and a facial had her entire body feeling limp as a wet noodle, and she was in heaven. All the tension of the past several days finally began to drift away.

By the time she sat down in the pedicure chair between her two cohorts she was positively oozing chill.

"Oh, my God, Bree. I cannot thank you enough for this. It is exactly what I needed."

"I'm so glad. All I wanted was to alleviate some stress for you."

"Well, mission accomplished." Sidney sighed and closed her eyes. "You know, now that tomorrow is the big day, all of the headaches just don't seem important anymore."

Bree and Jada both looked at her.

"I mean, the cake is being taken care of, thanks to you, Bree. And the dress fiasco is what it is. I can't change it. All I can do is put on the very lovely gown that was provided to me free of charge by the designer, and walk down the aisle."

"You know, Sid, I honestly do love this second gown even more than the first."

Sidney opened her eyes and looked at Bree.

"You really do?"

"Oh, I really do. I know you had your heart set on the first one that got shipped to Thailand by mistake. But this one... there's just something about it that screams beach wedding to me. Maybe it's the corded lace. It's so sweet. I just think it suits a beach wedding better than the fancier silk lace of the other dress."

"Well, I haven't seen this new dress yet," Jada chimed in. "But I agree with Bree about the corded lace. It does have a very sweet and innocent charm to it. Kind of like eyelet lace."

"And it's got the same high-low hem line that you loved about the original dress, so it's still going to show off your footwear to perfection. Plus it's strapless, which I think is perfect for a beach wedding. The other dress had straps and looked much more formal. It's going to beautiful, Sidney."

Sidney smiled at them both.

"Thanks, you guys."

"Don't thank us. We're only telling you the truth."

"Well, I appreciate it. Now, let's talk about something truly important." She looked over the available colors. "What do you guys think about a shimmery nude shade for my toes?"

"Oh, what about a shimmery overlay on top of French tips?" Jada offered.

"Ooh. That could be fun and pretty." Sidney looked at the manicurist doing her pedicure. "Let's do that."

The woman smiled at her and nodded.

"I love the whole barefoot on the beach thing, Sid." Bree grinned at her and chose a blush pink shade that perfectly matched her maid of honor dress. "I'm so excited to put on those barefoot sandals."

Sidney giggled.

"I know, I do love them. I'm so glad we found them. I was just going to go completely barefoot until I saw those."

"They are super cute. I know you're encouraging your guests to go barefoot too, so I think I'm going to have to buy some to wear to the wedding myself," Jada said.

Sidney looked at her neighbor and friend.

"I'm sorry. If Ike and I hadn't decided to keep the wedding party to just Adam and Bree, you would've been my first choice for a bridesmaid. You know that, right?"

Jada waved a dismissive hand.

"Oh, please. I'm not complaining. I'm perfectly happy to be co-hosting your bachelorette party tonight. I don't need to be a bridesmaid."

"Well, I appreciate your help with the festivities tonight more than you know," Bree told her.

"Not a problem. I'm happy to help."

"So, Jada, how's Pete doing? Isaac told me about Julieta."

"Yeah. It's so sad. And it's not like the doctors have given her a death sentence or anything. They haven't. It's just that Pete is taking it so hard. And he tries to be all strong for Julieta and Mateo, but it's like he has the weight of the world on his shoulders all the time, you know?"

"Yeah."

"And I've told him that I will help out in any way I can. Meals, transportation, whatever they need. But he's so set on doing everything himself. Like he doesn't want to ask anyone for help, and I'm just worried about him."

"It's gotta be rough."

"It is. His mom and Mateo are his world."

"Oh, I don't know about that. I think you and Charlie are becoming his world too."

Jada smiled, but there was a sadness to it.

"Yeah, I know. He loves us. I got really lucky when I met him. And I have you and Ike to thank for that. If you'd never moved in next door, my path never would've crossed with Pete's."

Sidney smiled at her. "Happy to help."

They all laughed.

"Listen, Jada, if any of you need anything. Anything at all, you call Ike and me, all right?"

"That goes for us too," Bree chimed in. "If Adam or I can help you or Pete in any way, don't hesitate."

"Thanks, you guys."

"You know," Bree continued, "we could load up Pete's freezer with dinners. All you or he or Julieta would have to do is pop them in the oven and bake. It would be a super big help to them."

"Oh, I love that idea." Sidney pointed at her. "Once we're back from our honeymoon, I could definitely contribute a couple of dinners a week."

"Yeah, me too. We can lighten Pete's load a lot."

"You guys are angels. I love that idea," Jada said. "And Pete will resist, because he's proud, but he will appreciate it too. Thank you."

"It's no problem, Jada. Really." Sidney lightly squeezed Jada's arm.

"Yeah, this is what friends are truly for," Bree added. "There's no need to thank us."

"Now that that's settled," Sidney turned to Bree. "What about you?"

"What do you mean?" Bree stared at her.

"I mean, what about you and Adam? How are you guys?"

"Exhausted. But we're functioning. Adam had a hard time going back to work after taking four weeks of paternity leave, but now we're settling into a routine. Sort of. I think Isla's day/night confusion is finally wearing off some."

"Oh, my God. I'm so sorry my wedding fell at such an inconvenient time for you guys. I'm sure Isla has you up at all hours of the night, and you've had to contend with Bridezilla over here."

"Oh, shut up. You have not been a Bridezilla. Besides going to the florist and shopping for wedding gowns with you, I haven't really done anything."

"You've done plenty, and you know it. And all I'm saying is, when we get back from our honeymoon, Auntie Sid is open for babysitting business. Anytime, day or night. Or even overnight."

"Ooh, girl, I am definitely taking you up on that offer. You're going to regret that!"

Bree's voice was sing-songy, and Sidney and Jada laughed.

Since the theme of the day was to treat themselves, a quick stop for ice cream cones followed their mani-pedi girl talk, and then they headed back to Sidney and Isaac's place to get set up for the bachelorette party.

"Well, don't you look radiant."

It was a statement, not a question, and Isaac's sexy grin as he said it made Sidney blush.

"Thank you. I feel radiant."

He reached out and threaded his fingers through her bouncy curls and gently pulled her forward. The kiss started out chaste enough, but quickly took a turn down Lusty Lane.

"Okay, that's enough of that, Detective!"

Bree sounded like she meant business.

"You two are pushing it being together right now. You, Mister, are due at my place soon, are you not?"

Isaac looked at Bree with surprised eyes.

"That is the plan that was laid out for me, yes."

"Then get to stepping. You two can't see each other anymore until you meet at the end of the aisle tomorrow. Now, go."

"What? Now, wait just a minute..."

"Go! You know the rules."

"But I don't agree with the rules!"

"Agh!"

Bree threw her hands up and headed for the kitchen to help Jada get the food ready.

Sidney and Isaac laughed when they were alone.

"I think we'd better do as she says. She seems pretty serious about it."

"Bree is not the boss of us, you know?"

Sidney giggled, and Ike kissed her again.

"Hey, did you get all your errands done?"

"Yep. Dropped off Mr. Hitchcock. Got all packed. Loaded my bags and yours into the car for tomorrow. I've got my wedding attire in a garment bag in the car. Plane tickets. Wedding rings. Check for the minister. It's all good."

"Wow." A sudden frisson of fear and excitement rippled through her belly like waves hitting the shore. "This is really happening."

"It sure as hell is. You getting cold feet?"

"My feet are warm, and fresh, and newly pedicured."

"Good. 'Cause I think I plan to do a little toe suckin' tomorrow night."

The look he gave her was downright wicked.

Heat flickered in his light grey eyes.

"Ooh." Desire gushed through her and pooled at the apex of her thighs. "Toes. That sounds interesting."

"Doesn't it though?"

He pulled her closer, the prelude to a kiss.

"Get out, Isaac!"

Bree tossed the rebuke over her shoulder as she walked past them.

Isaac sighed and rested his forehead on Sidney's.

"I can't wait to marry you tomorrow, darlin'. But this night apart just might do me in."

"I'm sure you'll be much too busy watching strippers tonight to give me a second thought."

"Oh, no! I made Adam promise there'd be no strippers tonight. I mean, can you imagine one of 'em trying to give me a lap dance? That would not go over well."

Sidney laughed out loud, and he grinned. He kissed her once more and then looked around the room.

"Hey, Bree?"

"Yes?"

"I'm leaving!"

"Good, go!" Bree grinned. "Have a fun bachelor party!"

When Isaac was finally gone, Sidney sat and watched Bree and Jada put up decorations all around her house. They wouldn't let her do anything to help, so she sat by and supervised and waited for her guests.

Ike's sister, Emily, arrived first, followed closely by his mom, Audrey, and baby Isla, whom she'd been babysitting so Bree could go to the spa.

"There's my little honorary flower girl!"

"She was a perfect angel all afternoon." Audrey handed over her granddaughter, and then rushed to Sidney for a hug.

"Thank you so much for watching her, Audrey."

"Are you kidding me? Thank you for asking!"

Sid's Aunt Bobbie, Erika and Tameka showed up next. As did her boss, Zoe.

"Sidney, your home is lovely!"

"Thank you, Zoe. Come meet everybody."

Bree's younger sister, Bronwyn arrived, and finally Detectives Gerri Miller and Keisha Harris.

They all pigged out on tiny pulled chicken sandwiches, individual cups of veggies and dip, caprese bites, and an assortment of macaroon cookies — all made lovingly by Bree's own hand, with a baking assist from Jada on the cookies.

The drinks were fruity and girly, the laughter was plentiful. And when the gifts were opened — sometimes racy, sometimes tasteful lingerie — the cat calls were loud and embarrassing. But Sidney loved every minute of it.

"Thank you all so much! I was expecting to play games. Isn't that what you do at a bridal shower?"

"Yes, that is what happens at a bridal shower," Bree confirmed.

"But this is a bachelorette party, Sid," Jada chimed in. "Where you play games of a different sort."

Sidney looked back and forth between them, a sinking feeling in her stomach.

"A different sort?"

The doorbell sounded.

"I'll get that!" Jada smiled broadly.

The pit in Sidney's stomach sank deeper.

A few seconds later Jada came back with a man in tow. He was carrying a large box under his arm.

"This delivery guy was at the door, Sid."

He was talk, dark, and muscular, and Sidney knew she was being set up.

"You guys. You didn't."

"I have a great big package for you, ma'am."

He pulled a boom box out of the package and hit play.

The music blared.

The stripper ripped off his shirt and started to gyrate.

The women screamed with delight.

Sidney's face hit her palm.

———

Isaac carried his wedding attire up to one of the spare bedrooms at Adam's house and hung the garment bag on the closet door.

Then he pulled out a notepad and pen and sat down to work on his wedding vows.

An hour later he was surrounded by wadded up pieces of paper.

A knock sounded at the bedroom door.

Adam stuck his head in just as a paper wad came sailing toward his head.

"Whoa! What the heck man? You come to my house and start trashing the place?"

"Sorry."

Adam picked up several paper wads and tossed them into the trashcan.

"What are you doing, Ike?"

"I'm trying to write my wedding vows."

"Wedding vows?"

"Yes."

"You haven't written your vows yet? Bree says Sidney's been done with hers for weeks. She's memorized them already."

Isaac tore off another sheet, balled it up and pitched it across the room.

"You're not helping, Adam."

"Well, you're getting married tomorrow morning, man!"

"I know that!"

"Oh, dude. You should've had this done by now."

"Will you go away and leave me alone so I can do this, please?"

"I can't. I came up here to tell you that your guests are arriving."

"What? Already?"

Isaac looked down at his watch.

"Already? Ike, it's time, man. Your bachelor party is happening now."

"Jeez."

He tossed the notepad and pen aside. He hated social gatherings with a deep and abiding passion. He'd only agreed to this bachelor party because Adam and Oliver seemed so disappointed when he said he didn't want one.

Of course, Oliver had offered to provide the entertainment for the evening, and Isaac could just imagine the type of loose party girls his little brother would bring. That's when he told them that he would only agree to a gathering if there were absolutely no girls of any kind — no strippers, no hookers, no "actresses" — whatsoever.

Oliver had called him a choice word or two, but Adam had finally made Oliver promise.

So the night would be filled with gentlemen's games, and Adam's man cave provided the perfect set up — a poker table, a pool table, an air hockey table, and a dartboard. He'd even thought to provide a case of cigars.

Isaac followed Adam down the stairs to the main floor, and then down into the basement, where a long table to the side of the large room had been piled high with three different types of chicken wings, two kinds of dip, chips, pretzels and six pizza boxes that made Isaac's stomach growl.

There was every kind of soda he could think of, plus an ample supply of non-alcoholic beer.

Isaac glanced around and spotted his grandad, Sterling, and his brother, Oliver, Sid's brother, Simon, and her uncle Frank already milling around.

"On the big screen, Ike," Adam pointed to the giant screen TV mounted on the wall, "you have your choice of porn or sports. It's your party, so you choose."

Isaac looked at him hoping his expression conveyed everything.

"What do you think?"

Adam grinned and shrugged a shoulder.

"Hey, you could learn something you want to take on your honeymoon, you know?"

Isaac smirked at him.

"Very funny. My future brother-in-law and my future father-in-law will be here. Sports, Adam. Put it on sports."

"All right. Sports it is."

In no time at all, the man cave filled up with more guys — Pete and Gavin, along with a few others from the PD, like Gary Barker and Ben Dale. Hiroshi Sato and Emmett Fox. Ike's former partner, Don Marsh even showed up. Isaac's dad, Brock, came in last, along with Sid's father, Carlton.

The room was loud and crowded. Both things that Isaac hated.

The food was attacked, and Isaac sat with his back to the wall and chowed down on a slice of pizza and some of the hot wings.

In his heart of hearts, he knew that he was trying to make himself smaller. Not an easy task when you stood six foot four, but the crowded room made him uncomfortable.

"I see you."

He looked to his side, where Sterling took a seat beside him with his own plate.

"That line was treacherous, wasn't it?"

Isaac nodded. "Yes, it was."

No one but his grandad would describe the buffet line as treacherous, but Isaac understood completely because he felt the same way. Too many people reaching past you and around you, bumping into you, rubbing shoulders.

Nightmare.

He glanced over at Sterling now.

"Hey, Grandad. You know... I'm touched by you wanting to move here for me. Truly, I am. But moving to a new state, a strange city. That's a big deal. I wouldn't want to be responsible for taking you away from your daily routine and the surroundings that are familiar and comforting to you."

Sterling smiled at him.

"Oh, but you're not responsible for taking me away from anything. This is something I've been thinking about doing ever since you first came to visit me months ago."

"It is?"

"It most certainly is. Isaac, we've lost so much valuable time together. Time that I could've been teaching you everything you need to know to safely navigate this world with our unique issues."

"Well, I can't argue with that, because it's true."

"It is true. And I don't plan on punching my ticket to heaven any time soon, but let's be practical here. I'm an old man now. I've only got so many good years left. I want to spend those years getting to know all of my grandchildren better, not just you. But I also want to spend those years teaching you everything I know about our abilities, and about our psychic heritage."

Isaac smiled at him.

"And guess what?"

"What's that?"

"When I was packing my things, I recently came across some items I think you would be interested in."

"What kind of items, Grandad?"

"Things like diaries and letters that were written by Etta Sterling and Atticus Hawthorne."

Excitement sparked in Isaac's chest.

Those were two important links in their psychic heritage. Etta Sterling was his grandad's mother's mother. And Atticus Hawthorne was Etta Sterling's father. Both of them supposedly had the same psychic powers that Isaac and his grandad shared.

"Seriously?"

He nearly salivated at the thought of getting his hands on those journals and letters. They could contain valuable information about where their abilities came from. Isaac would love to be able to trace this psychic thing back through his family line.

"It's time I passed them down to you. They're things I think you should have."

Isaac was quiet for a moment.

"Grandad, if moving here is something you're sure you want to do, you'll have my complete support. You can even stay with Sid and me until we find you a place."

Sterling smiled.

"Well, that'd be just fine. Thank you for the offer. It's going to be great."

Sterling got up and walked away, and Isaac realized he'd just invited his grandfather to stay with them without consulting Sidney first.

"Crap."

As the party stretched into the night, Isaac got wrapped up in a serious poker game with all of his old poker buddies from the PD — Gary Barker, Ben Dale and his now-retired former partner, Don Marsh. Adam and Oliver battled it out on the air hockey table while Pete and Hiroshi played a rousing game of pool, with Sid's uncle Frank, Simon, and his dad, Brock, watching all the action and talking. Gavin and Emmett were playing darts and talking trash.

Everyone appeared to be having a good time, and Isaac was actually glad he'd let his brothers talk him into this.

———

Simon stood in the midst of the bachelor party with a non-alcoholic beer in his hand. He'd started out watching the pool game going on between Ike's partner, Pete, and some Asian dude named Hiroshi.

Uncle Frank was still riveted on the pool action, but Simon's attention was pulled to the large flat screen and the baseball game going on. He turned toward it to get a better view, and then he felt it.

He was being watched.

That was always a creepy feeling.

His gaze drifted left toward the poker game, and then right.

He spotted Carlton off to the side of the room, standing alone and simply watching.

Watching him.

Simon sighed and tried to ignore him. He turned back to the game hoping the man would take the hint.

Simon didn't even know why Carlton had bothered to come.

He wasn't actually participating in any of the games or conversations going on. He clearly wasn't helping Ike to celebrate his last night as a single man. So what the hell was he even doing here?

That thought made him roll his eyes at himself.

"You know what he's doing here, you idiot," he thought to himself. *"He's here because you're here."*

Simon rolled his shoulders to try and relieve some of the tension there. Why did Carlton's presence make him so angry?

He could see his sister's face. See her eyes imploring him to have a civil conversation with Carlton. She'd said he was dying.

Simon pushed those thoughts from his mind and focused on the game. He stepped over to the black leather couch. More specifically, to the coffee table in front of the couch, where a pizza box had been placed.

He grabbed a slice, took a bite, and sat down to watch the game.

He was quickly engrossed in it. So much so that when a commercial break came, he glanced to his right and noticed for the first time that Carlton was quietly sitting next to him.

Simon sighed and took a swig of near-beer.

"I feel like you're stalking me, man."

Carlton nodded. "Yeah. I feel like I'm stalking you too, so... I guess that's about right.

A tense silence muscled its way in between them and sat down.

Then they both spoke at once.

"Sid tells me that..."

"Look, I know that..."

They stopped and stared at each other.

Carlton gestured to him.

"You go. Please."

Simon wiped his hands on a napkin.

"Sid says you're uh... you're sick?"

A tight smile briefly passed Carlton's lips.

"You know, it's funny. I never think of it that way. That I'm sick, or ill." He paused for a few seconds. "But yeah. I'm dying."

Simon looked him in the eyes.

He remembered those eyes so well. Remembered the way they'd crinkle whenever his daddy smiled. Especially when he smiled at him.

Simon's jaw clinched tight.

"Of what?"

"The technical name has so many syllables I haven't even attempted to learn it. But suffice it to say that the tumor is large, and it's wrapped around my brain stem."

Simon frowned, his medical mind taking over.

"What? Like a brain stem glioma, or a medulloblastoma, or something like that?"

"Oh, what does the name matter?" Carlton grinned, but there was no joy in it. "It's still killing me."

"Well, it matters a lot. Both of those conditions are more common in children, but not unheard of in adults. It could mean that..."

"My son, the *doctor.*" Carlton interrupted him. "The *surgeon.* Air Force Major."

His tone was full of pride. His smile was full of affection.

The same affection-filled smile Simon remembered from when he was a child.

That memory had him gut-punched.

Carlton, still smiling, shook his head.

"You really made something of yourself, didn't you?"

The pride in Carlton's voice pissed him off.

"Yeah, I did. Without any input from you."

Simon's voice was tight, and he tried hard to remember that they were in the middle of Ike's bachelor party and he did not want to ruin that. But he had some things to say to this man.

"Sid and I both worked our asses off after you made us just another statistic. Just another couple of black kids in the inner city growing up with no father. Lucky for us, Uncle Frank was always around."

Carlton nodded.

"I know that I'll never be able to apologize enough, Simon. And I don't expect you to believe this, but... I loved your mother so much."

"Really?"

"Yes. But I was so unprepared to be a husband and a father back then. I was so young. I didn't know how to be a steady kind of guy. I couldn't hold a 9 to 5 back then. I couldn't..."

"Couldn't keep your dick in your pants?"

Simon glared at him.

The tense pause dragged on a beat.

"Yeah. There were women. I'm not proud of that. I'm not proud of anything I did back then, except make you and Sidney. I spent most of my adult life running from the things I should've been protecting and building. Now, when that life is being taken from me all I want is to see what I've lost. See the things I could've been a part of if I hadn't been so stupid."

To Simon's horror, Carlton's voice broke and his eyes welled with tears. He watched them spill over and roll slowly down his father's face.

Shit.

The lump in his own throat angered him, and it shook something loose. Some stray bit of compassion. He tried to swallow it down.

"Let me ask you a question, Carlton."

"Anything."

Carlton wiped his face with the back of his hand.

Simon fixed his eyes on his father's.

"If you'd never gotten sick. If you weren't dying... would you have still come sniffing around eventually?"

Carlton's response was immediate.

"Yes."

And he sounded so certain. That shocked Simon.

"Because you know what I've discovered? Dying makes you brave. There were so many times throughout the years that I thought about reaching out, seeing if your lives had room for me. I always wanted to be part of your lives, but... so much time had passed, and I was afraid to ask. But the diagnosis." He paused and wiped his face again. "Dying makes you brave."

Simon wasn't sure what he'd expected Carlton to say. But that hadn't been it.

"How long do they give you?"

"Three months. If I'm lucky."

"I want to see your scans. Will you let me look at them?"

Carlton shrugged a shoulder. "If that's what you want."

Simon nodded. He'd get his doctor's information and make the request on Monday. For now though, he took another slice of pizza and slid the box over Carlton's way.

Carlton looked at him with a question in his eyes. Then he grabbed a napkin and took a slice of pizza.

"You a baseball fan, Carlton?"

"I prefer basketball, but... if you're offering me the chance to watch a game with my son, I'll take it."

They turned to the ballgame then and ate in silence. After a few moments, Carlton leaned over close.

"So what do you really think of this Isaac character? Are you as cool with him as you seem? Is he good to Sidney?"

Simon grinned and looked at him.

"Honestly, I thought Ike was an odd duck at first. But now, yes, we are cool. And yes, he is very good to Sidney. He treats her like a queen. Worships her dirty bath water. He's a good man."

"His family sure seems to like her."

"They all love her. I've met every one of them well before now, and I've never seen the first hint of racism anywhere. Not even from his dad, who can come off as stern sometimes. They're good people, Carlton. She'll be well taken care of."

"What about you? You got a significant other? Do I have any grandkids running around somewhere?"

Simon grinned and shook his head.

"Not yet."

"What you waiting on?"

"The right woman might be nice."

"Yeah, well, when you find her, don't be like your old man, you hear me? I've shown you what *not* to do. You step up. You treat her right."

Simon looked him over and wondered for the first time in a long time, what it might've been like to have a dad growing up.

"Yeah, I hear you."

18

The bachelor party finally broke up near one in the morning, and Isaac was close to 400 bucks richer. He told his poker buddies not to worry though, because he and Sidney would put their lost cash to good use on their honeymoon.

When the last stragglers — Pete and Hiroshi — were finally out the door, Isaac turned to Adam.

"Should we clean up?"

"Nope. The maid will do that in the morning."

"The maid," Isaac mused. "Must be nice."

Adam only grinned at him.

"Well, in that case, I'm going up to bed. Should've been in bed. Like Grandad."

Sterling had gone to bed after eating some food. Said he would leave the partying to the youngsters.

"All right. Hey, what about your vows though, man? You never finished them."

Isaac sighed and tried not to let the panic creep into his stomach.

"I'm going to wing it."

"You're going to wing it?"

"Yep."

"Are you nuts?"

"No, I'm tired. I'm sleepy, I've got a big day tomorrow, and I'm not going to stress over my vows. I'm going to look into Sidney's eyes tomorrow and I'm going to tell her what's in my heart. Simple as that."

Adam looked slightly stunned.

"Okay."

Isaac took a breath. Was he nuts?

"Okay. Goodnight."

"G'night."

He headed up the stairs to his designated guest room and stripped out of his clothes. As he crawled into bed he grabbed his cellphone and did the one thing he'd been wanting to do all night long.

He called his Sidney.

"Isaac?"

"Hey, darlin'. You still up?"

He glanced around the well-appointed guest room and felt nothing but loneliness. Especially when he heard her sweet voice.

"I'm just crawling into bed now. Not that I'll be able to sleep much. Our bed feels very cold and lonely without you."

"Tell me about it. I feel like a stranger in a strange land over here."

"I'm sure Bree and Adam have done everything they can to make you comfortable in their guest room."

"Oh, they have. And Grandad's just across the hall in the other guest room. But I'm missing your sweet-smelling, soft, warm body. I got nothing to curl up to over here but a pillow, and that is no kind of substitute for you."

Sidney giggled, and the sound of it made him smile.

"It's just one night. And think about it... this time tomorrow, you and I will be Mr. and Mrs. You'll be completely stuck with me then."

"I can't wait to be completely and totally stuck with you, forever. But what I'd like to know is who came up with this rule that the bride and groom aren't allowed to see each other the day before the wedding? That's a load of superstitious crap right there. Kinda like curses."

He could hear the frustration in his own voice, but it couldn't be helped. Sidney laughed at him.

"I've missed you today too, baby. But I think the tradition goes back to when marriages were arranged, and the families didn't want the couple to see each other beforehand out of fear they'd back out if they saw who they were marrying. Terrifying prospect if you ask me."

"Aw, hell. And here we are, a hundred years later, still suffering 'cause they weren't allowed to choose for themselves? Forget that, I'm coming home."

He was totally joking. Unless, of course, she liked the idea.

"Isaac! You can't."

So much for that idea.

"Well, why the hell not? It's not like it's actually bad luck or anything."

"How do you know that? And after everything that's already gone wrong with this wedding, and the unwelcome family surprises? I just don't want to tempt fate, or... you know... piss it off."

Isaac's righteous indignation deflated like she'd popped his bubble with a giant spitball.

"It's just one night, baby. And think about how much sweeter tomorrow night will be when we're finally married and alone, and on our way to... wherever our honeymoon is."

Isaac laughed out loud.

"Nice try, darlin', but I'm still not telling you where we're going."

"But I don't even know if I've packed the right things, Ike! You could at least give me a hint."

"I did give you a hint. I told you that all you really need is a bikini and a toothbrush. Mostly just the toothbrush, 'cause I don't expect to let you leave the room too often."

Sidney's sexy giggle connected with his dick, and he stifled a groan.

"So, since you're making me endure this torture of sleeping without you tonight, I was wondering…"

His voice trailed off as he wondered exactly how to ask this question. He had no clue how men actually set these things up.

"Yes?"

"Well, do you remember back when we first got together? Um, back when I was still very awkward about… well, about sex and being intimate, and all that?"

"Yes."

He could hear the curiosity in her voice, and it only made him more nervous. He licked his lips and softly cleared his throat before trying again.

"Well, you said that if there was ever anything that I wanted to try, I should just tell you?"

"Isaac, is there something special you're wanting to try when we're on our honeymoon?"

"Well actually…"

"Maybe a little anal play perhaps?"

Heart stopped.

Thoughts gone.

Words forgotten.

"A… a-a little what now?"

Had she said those words, or had he imagined them? Was she still talking?

"…I mean, I've never done that before, but I know you're really kind of an ass man, and I think…"

"Sidney, stop! Talking. Please. I-I can't think when you say things like that."

Her soft, sexy laughter only made things worse, and he repositioned the wood between his legs.

"Isaac, you're not being bashful right now, are you?"

"A little. I mean, this isn't exactly a normal conversation. And that's not what I was getting at, although now it's all I can think about."

Sidney laughed even harder.

"So, what were you getting at then?"

"Well, I was hinting at... you know... phone sex."

"Ohhh!"

"Yeah."

"Well, do you want to know what I'm wearing?"

Her voice was suddenly breathy and hyper-sexy, and Isaac just had to laugh. And he was certain that was the wrong response.

"What's funny? I'm trying to start the phone sex conversation here."

"How do you switch gears like that so quickly? Doesn't anything ever faze you, darlin'?"

"Only scary bad things. But stuff like this? Sexy, secret stuff between you and me? That doesn't faze me one bit, Isaac. Why should I be embarrassed or shy with you, baby? You're the man I love, the man I want to share all of me with, body and soul. I want to do everything I can to give you physical pleasure. Especially knowing that you were deprived of it for so long. Tell me what you want, and I'll do my best to give it to you."

Her voice was low and sultry.

Isaac swallowed and wished like hell that they were together.

"God, I wish we were in the same house right now. Are you sure you won't let me come home? Not even for a few hours? No one would have to know but you and me."

Sidney laughed at him, and Isaac grinned.

"Baby?"

"Yes, darlin'?"

"What are you wearing?"

Isaac chuckled.

"I'm just wearing my boxer shorts."

"Boxer shorts and nothing else?"

"That's right."

"So that amazing man chest of yours is on full display?"

"Yes, but I wasn't aware that it was amazing."

"You mean I've never told you how much I appreciate your broad, strong chest, or the perfect amount of hair dusted over your pecs?"

"Um... no."

"Or your chiseled eight pack of abs, and that enticing V at your hips that turns me stupid?"

"The what at the where?

"Or the veins that run down your well-defined arms to your masculine hands that drive me crazy?"

Her voice was low and sexy, and Isaac was suddenly hard as hell.

"Uh... no. You haven't."

"Mmm. Well, now you know."

Isaac's mouth was dry.

"Are... are you... I mean, were you serious just now, or was that all pretend for the phone sex?"

Sidney laughed at him, and Isaac felt about as foolish as a tit on a bull.

"Can't both things be true, Ike?"

"Huh?"

"Yes, I was sexing it up for the sake of our little game here. But every single word I said was the truth. In my opinion, you are the sexiest man I've ever known, baby. For all the reasons I just stated, and then some."

"Wow. Really?"

"Yes, really."

He blew air through his lips.

"I guess I'm very bad at this, huh?"

"It's your first time. You'll get the hang of it."

He could hear the smile in her voice, and it made him grin.

"So, tell me... how was your party?"

"Oh, you know. Food, lingerie, male strippers."

He heard every word, but he was only concerned about one.

"Lingerie?"

"Yeah, I got some pretty sexy stuff as gifts. A few of them I'd like to add to my suitcase before we leave tomorrow. Maybe give you a little fashion show on our honeymoon."

"Yes, please. I think we can definitely find time to slip a few things into your luggage tomorrow."

She laughed at him, and he grinned at the sound of it.

"And what'd you do after everybody left your party?"

Sidney sighed, and the sound of it over the phone made him even more horny than he already was.

"Well, it's been a very long day, so I just locked the door, told Erika goodnight, stripped off my clothes and crawled into bed."

"Oh, yeah?"

"Mmm hmm."

"Sooo, you're uh... naked right now?"

He could almost hear her smile over the phone.

"Well, not completely. See, you, bad boy, left a t-shirt draped over the chair instead of putting it in the hamper."

"Oh. Sorry about that."

"I'm not. Because it smells like you. And I missed you, so I put it on."

"Huh. So, underneath the t-shirt, I'd find...?"

"Nothing but me, baby. Ready and waiting for you."

Isaac groaned.

She was really good at this phone sex thing.

"You are killing me here."

Sidney softly laughed, and it was the sexiest thing he'd heard all night.

It sparked both his imagination and his boldness.

"I'd like to run my hand up the back of your thigh right now. Take a handful of that ass and squeeze it tight."

"Ooh. I like it when you do that."

He could hear the delight in Sidney's voice.

"Yeah?"

"Uh huh."

"Tell me what else you like, darlin'."

He laid back and got comfortable, and he smiled as he listened to her tell him all the dirty things she wanted him to do.

19

*S*idney woke up bright and early on Saturday morning. The birds were singing.

The sun was shining.

The sky was crystal blue.

It was going to be a glorious day.

She thought about Isaac and smiled. Their phone sex session last night had turned out to be an incredibly sexy adventure. An adventure that had been very satisfying for both of them. Who knew?

She'd never done anything like that with anyone else before, and she'd been pleasantly surprised to discover that dirty-talking Isaac was quite a turn on. Maybe it was because he was normally so buttoned up and careful all the time. But on the phone last night, he'd completely let go with her.

It was the same whenever they were together. She loved being the one person in the world that he could routinely let go with. The person he could be most intimate with. The person who could touch him the deepest.

She got up and showered, paying special attention to her mountain of wayward curls. If there was ever a day she needed them to be on point, it was today. By the time she was done with them, her curls were laying in beautifully sculpted ringlets that danced around her head and shoulders, ready to be styled in whatever manner she chose.

"Sid, I made eggs and toast. Some coffee. You hungry?"

Her cousin, Erika stood in the bedroom doorway.

Sidney shook her head.

"I think I'm too excited to eat right now."

"You should try to eat a little something. You don't want to pass out halfway down the aisle, do you?"

She had to laugh at that visual.

"Okay. Maybe just some eggs."

She accepted the small plate of eggs and took a few bites, but her nervous stomach just wasn't having it.

The doorbell rang. It was a sound that would occur many times before the morning was over.

Jada arrived first, ready to help with hair and makeup.

Bree came next, followed by Aunt Bobbie and Tameka.

Her bedroom and bathroom were filled with happy chatter as they all helped her get ready. In no time at all, her hair and makeup were perfect.

She'd chosen to wear her hair pulled back on one side, secured with a silver hair clip that sported a silk orchid on top. She had chosen it specifically to match her bridal bouquet — Esperance roses, with a cascade of white phalaenopsis orchids with dark pink centers trailing downward.

They kept her makeup light and natural to capture the sun-soaked beach feeling. A bit of rose gold shimmer on her eyelids and a bronzy tone for her blush. Nude lipstick with just a hint of gold sparkle to the lip gloss.

It was flawless and stunning.

"Oh, Jada! You've made me look like a princess."

"No, no, girlfriend. You naturally look like a princess. I just helped make you sparkle, that's all."

"Okay now, before you step into your gown, I want to give you something."

Sidney turned to her Aunt Bobbie, who was pulling something out of her purse.

"I told Bree that I wanted to take care of your something old and blue."

She pulled out a dainty bangle bracelet and slipped it over Sidney's wrist.

Sidney brought her wrist close and studied the bracelet's intricate details. It was pink enamel with white and blue flowers that were outlined in gold.

"Aunt Bobbie, it's lovely! Thank you."

"It was your mother's."

Sidney gasped and looked at her.

"It was?"

"She bought it herself with her own babysitting money, back when we were in high school. She saw it in a drugstore window and thought it was the prettiest thing. She had to have it."

Sidney rotated the bracelet around her wrist, still studying it.

"I think I vaguely remember her wearing this when I was little. I wonder why she stopped?"

"I don't know."

"I didn't even think about it after she died."

"Well, I'm ashamed to say that I took it from her jewelry box after she died. I should've left it for you. But it just made me think back on that time when we were kids, and I was grieving, and so I..."

"No, Aunt Bobbie." Sidney reached out and took her arm. "You loved her. You deserve to have something to remember her by; don't apologize for that."

"I have many things to remember my sister by, Sidney. Namely you and your brother. I don't need that bracelet. It's why I brought it. I wanted to give it to you. I want you to have it, honey."

Sidney hugged her and kissed her cheek.

"Dawn would be so proud of you."

"Thank you, Auntie."

"Okay, no tears! No tears. We do not have time to redo your makeup."

Laughter went around the room, and Sidney dabbed at her eyes with a tissue.

"So, I have your something new. And now seems to be the perfect time for it," Jada said, handing her a small, delicate, white, linen hanky with lace trim. The initials ST were stitched in the corner in cream thread.

"Oh, Jada, that's beautiful. It's got my new initials. Thank you."

"I figured it would probably come in handy today."

"Good call," Sidney said, and used it to dab at her eyes.

"And I have your something borrowed." Bree handed her a small box.

Sidney opened it to find a pair of small, dangly, flower-shaped, diamond earrings. They had to be at least three carats total.

"Bree!"

It was a startled whisper.

"I can't wear these!"

"Yes you can. Since the corded lace of your gown is in a flower pattern, I thought these earrings would look darling with it. They were a gift from Adam for our first wedding anniversary. I want you to wear them."

Sidney looked her matron-of-honor in the eyes, speechless.

Bree pointed a finger at her.

"Don't you do it! Don't you cry again, Sidney."

They all laughed, and Sidney dabbed at her eyes again.

"You guys are all too much."

"We just want your wedding day to be perfect, Sid." Bree took the box from her hands and proceeded to put the earrings in Sidney's ear lobes.

"All right, I'll wear them. But I am giving them back to you before we leave on our honeymoon!"

"Fine, fine."

"Okay," Jada said, smiling. "Time for the dress."

Twenty minutes later, Sidney stood alone in her bedroom, staring at herself in the full-length mirror on the back of the door. The other ladies had all filed out to give her a moment to herself before time to go.

She had to admit, this new dress really did look stunning.

A high-low tea-length silhouette with a strapless, semi-sweetheart neckline. She'd dressed it up at the waist with a rhinestone belt from the designer, and the sparkle of it matched the rhinestone starfish that embellished the barefoot sandals on her perfectly pedicured feet.

All she needed now was a bouquet and a groom.

A soft knock sounded on her bedroom door and Simon poked his head in, eyes closed.

"You decent?"

Sidney laughed and placed her hands on his face.

"Yes, Simon, I'm right here."

"Oh." He opened his eyes and grinned. Then he stepped in and looked her over. "Wow. You look pretty as a picture, sis."

"Thank you."

He shook his head and smirked at her.

"Barefoot on the beach. Nobody but my sister would want to get married that way."

Sidney laughed and stuck out her foot, showing off her pedicure and the blinged-out foot jewelry.

"What is that?" Simon laughed.

"What? They're called a barefoot sandals. Aren't they cute?"

"It's... they're perfect for your beach wedding, Sid. Ike is going to faint when he sees you coming down the aisle."

"I hope not! Although that might be funny."

Simon laughed.

Sidney took a moment to look over his attire at well. Light tan linen pants and a pale pink dress shirt, sleeves rolled up a notch, untucked for effect. A straw fedora cocked at just the right angle on top of his head. At the moment, he was wearing a pair of black flip flops on his feet, but those would come off for the ceremony.

"You look great too."

"Why, thank you." He grinned at her. "Oh, by the way, there's a big box on the table out here. When she left, Bree said not to forget it?"

"Yes. That's my bouquet."

"Ah. Well, are you ready?"

"Ready as I'll ever be."

She slipped on a pair of rhinestone flip flop shoes for the ride to the beach. Since the reception was in a restaurant she would need the footwear after the ceremony. She grabbed her breath-taking bouquet on the way out the door.

Everyone else had already gone ahead, so it was just her and Simon in the back of the cream-colored limo on the drive to the beach.

"Listen, Sid, I want you to know that I talked with Carlton last night at the bachelor party."

Sidney looked at him.

"How'd it go?"

Simon sighed.

"It was good. We cleared the air, I think. He apologized for a lot of things. I'm going to have a look at his scans. Show them to a neurosurgeon colleague of mine." He paused and glanced over at her. "Might be a lost cause, but... it couldn't hurt."

"No, it couldn't. Did he ask you to do that?"

Simon shook his head.

"I asked if he would mind."

"I think that's great, Simon. I actually wouldn't mind having a little more time with Carlton, you know? Is that weird? After the way he walked out on Mom and pretended we didn't exist for so many years?"

"It's not weird. It's normal."

"You feel that way too?"

He was silent for a moment, and Sidney wondered what he was thinking.

"Yeah, I kinda do."

Relief washed through her system. But she wasn't certain that was the right emotion.

"Are we pathetic statistic kids with daddy issues?"

Simon smiled and tried not to laugh, making Sidney giggle.

"Maybe you are, but I'm not."

That made her laugh even more. She reached over and took her brother's hand.

"I love you, Simon. You're a good big brother."

"You make a pretty good brother yourself, Sid."

She punched him in the arm, and he laughed.

"No, I love you too. As little sisters go, you're okay."

"Gee, thanks."

They arrived at the beach right on time for the very strictly choreographed ceremony. When she stepped out of the limo, she could see the driftwood arch set up in the sand, just in the distance, adorned with sprays of her chosen flowers.

Their guests were all in place.

The music began — "Marry Me," by Train.

Isaac, with his best man, Adam, following behind, stepped into the aisle of sand and made his way to the arch to join the minister.

He was decked out in his cream-colored linen suit and untucked white dress shirt. The lapel of his jacket sported a small starfish and orchid boutonnière. The hem of his pants had been cuffed up, protecting them from the sand and surf, and showing off his sexy feet.

Adam wore a similar ensemble — the cream linen pants with

rolled up cuffs, and the untucked white dress shirt, minus the jacket.

As the music played, Simon and Sidney made their way to the top of the stairs that led down to the sand, and she watched Bree in her pretty, pale pink dress so similar to her own, slowly make her way down the aisle carrying a small bouquet of Esperance roses.

When Bree took her place in front of the arch, Sidney looked at Simon.

"That's my cue."

"Let's get you married."

Simon hooked her arm into his and led her down the steps and over to their stretch of sand.

Ahead of them, Jabari, her cousin's four-year-old son, executed his bell-ringer duties to perfection. Prompted by the venue's event planner at the precise moment, the little boy walked down the aisle ringing his bell, just as the music changed — "In My Arms," by Johnnyswim.

"The bride is coming! The bride is coming! The bride is coming!"

His sweet little voice drew a combination of *"aww"* and delighted laughter from their guests, and everyone got to their feet.

Sidney and Simon started down the aisle.

Butterflies took flight in Sidney's belly.

She listened to the words of the song, to the promises the couple were making to each other.

In her heart and soul, she was making all those same promises to Isaac.

Isaac.

He looked so handsome with the sunshine painting golden streaks in his honey blond hair. The top two buttons of his untucked white shirt were open, hinting at the spectacular chest and broad shoulders she knew were hidden underneath.

Her gaze found his.

Her heart fluttered.

She wasn't certain exactly how she'd reached the arch in the sand. She certainly didn't remember walking.

But when Isaac took her hands and she looked up into his bright grey eyes, she knew she was home.

———

He'd known that his emotions would be riding high.

He'd known that she would look more beautiful than he'd ever seen her.

But what Isaac hadn't been prepared for were the tears that stung his eyes the instant he saw her coming toward him.

In the flirty white lace dress that showed off her amazing legs, she was a goddess.

She was the sunlight.

His Sidney.

His.

He had waited so long for this. Waited so long for *her*.

For this love. For this gift. For *this* woman.

His chest swelled with love, pride, gratefulness.

Simon kissed Sidney's cheek and then turned to Isaac.

"You take care of my baby sister, Ike."

"You know I will."

He barely got the words out past the lump of jumbled feelings stuck in his throat.

Simon stepped away and took a seat next to their aunt and uncle in the front row.

Isaac took Sidney's hand and looked down into her eyes.

"You are everything," he whispered.

A tear hit his cheek, and he didn't give a damn.

Sidney reached up and wiped it away.

"Blue skies, baby," she whispered back. "Nothing but blue skies and starry nights from this day forward."

Isaac kissed the palm of her hand, and then led her to the driftwood arch and the minister.

He tried to pay attention and listen as the minister began the ceremony, leading them through a prayer and the significance of the institution of marriage. But the only thing on Isaac's mind, the only thing he could concentrate on was the breathtaking woman beside him. When the minister finally had them face each other, his heart nearly leapt from his chest.

"Isaac and Sidney have chosen to write their own vows today. Isaac?"

This was it.

His heart began to pound.

Why hadn't he taken the time to write anything?

What was it he'd told Adam? That he'd look into Sid's eyes and wing it?

He took a deep breath and looked into her eyes now.

The love and serenity he found there filled his heart and calmed his nerves.

He lightly squeezed her hands and swallowed down his anxiety.

"We spoke on the phone long before we ever met in person. The sound of your voice that first night, it seeped in and grabbed hold of some lonely, frightened part of me. I have never been so happy about making a wrong number phone call in all my life."

Sidney giggled.

Their guests chuckled with her, and Isaac grinned.

"I was in prison when we met, Sidney. Trapped inside my own body, afraid of the monsters inside me. But I told you all about those monsters, and I shared every dark secret with you. And you chose to stay and love me anyway. You touched me, literally, and brought sunshine instead of pain. You freed me from that dark prison, and you've changed my whole world."

Tears fell.

He couldn't hide them.

"I promise that I will never lose sight of what you mean to me. I will never take your love for granted. I promise that I will always run to your rescue, even though you're more than capable of rescuing yourself. And I promise to always put you first, to always cherish you. And to always stay out of the kitchen and not attempt to cook by myself."

Laughter came from the crowd of guests, but Sidney was wiping tears as she giggled.

Isaac caught one of her tears with his thumb, and she reached up and wiped his damp cheek.

"Oh, Isaac. You say that I changed your world, but you've changed mine just as much. I was living in my own kind of prison when I met you. Scared and alone in a strange place, afraid of my own shadow. Hiding from the world. And then you found me. A friendly, caring voice on the other end of the line."

Her voice broke, and Isaac lightly squeezed her hand, encouraging her to go on.

"You saved my life in so many ways. Your love has made me brave. Because of your love, I'm not afraid anymore. I've learned how to stand on my own two feet. How to stand up for myself. And I never would have gotten there if I'd never met you."

Isaac reached out and wiped another of her tears.

"I promise to love you more each day. I promise to always hold you close. I promise to always be your safe place, and your shield. I promise to cherish you, and to always put your needs ahead of my own. Oh! And I promise to do the cooking so that you don't poison us, or burn the house down."

This time, even the minister chuckled.

When the laughter subsided, the minister quietly cleared his throat.

"And now, to make it all official... may we have the rings, please?"

Isaac turned to Adam, who dug the rings out of his pocket and handed them over.

A matching set of white gold perfection that featured a brushed side and a polished side for his ring, and a brushed side and a diamond side for hers. Each ring had the same phrase engraved inside — *Blue skies and starry nights.*

It was their new catch phrase.

Their motto for the future.

Their code words for living happily ever after.

They slipped the rings on each other's fingers.

"Do you, Isaac Greer Taylor, take thee, Sidney Marie Fairchild, to be your lawfully wedded wife?"

"Yes, I do."

"And do you, Sidney Marie Fairchild, take thee, Isaac Greer Taylor, to be your lawfully wedded husband?"

"I absolutely do."

"Then, by the power vested in me by the great state of Ohio, I now pronounce you husband and wife. Those whom God has joined together, let no man put asunder. You may kiss your bride."

The music began — "This Will Be," by Natalie Cole — and Isaac gently took Sidney's face in his hands and kissed her reverently. Then, never breaking their kiss, he took her in his arms and turned, dipping her deeply backwards.

The polite applause from their friends and family erupted into loud cheers, whistles and more laughter.

"Way to go, Mutant!" Adam called out.

Sidney's laugh was breathless, and her champagne-colored eyes sparkled at him.

He righted her on her feet, both of them smiling through fresh tears.

"Ladies and gentlemen," the minister said. "I present to you for the first time ever, Mr. and Mrs. Isaac Taylor."

Isaac had no clue what made him do it.

And he could tell by the look in her eyes that she was

completely shocked when he took her hand and started to dance to the music.

Their crowd of friends and family erupted again in shocked joy.

Sidney started to dance with him.

He spun her around and around, and then they danced down the aisle and all the way over to the Sunset Terrace restaurant for the reception.

———

They feasted on an elegant array of appetizers, including caviar topped scallops, fried oysters, bacon wrapped dates, mini spring rolls, deep fried asparagus spears, and mini Perch fish tacos.

They mingled with their family and friends and took tons of beautiful pictures in the rose garden and on the beach.

But mostly, they boogied.

Sidney had insisted on two separate dance floors for their reception. One for their guests, and a small private one nearby, roped off with bright yellow police tape, just for her and Isaac.

He'd asked for a space where he could dance with her and not be worried about anyone else accidentally touching him, so she made it happen. And they put it to good use.

When he'd told her weeks ago that he wanted to dance at their wedding, he wasn't kidding.

"Hey, Lieu, tell me something," Pete said, staring at Isaac, but addressing their boss.

"What?"

"Did you know Ike could dance?"

Gavin shook his head. "I'm shocked that he would allow himself to dance."

"Me too! But I'm also surprised that he even knows how."

"I'm sitting right here, y'all." Isaac grinned at them.

"We know," Pete said, looking him over. "You're not half bad."

"Gee, thanks."

Sidney laughed at them, but she'd heard similar conversations between others during their reception.

"Ike dances? Who the fuck knew?" from Oliver, talking to Emily.

"Who is that normal acting young man on the dance floor, and what has he done with our son?" from Brock speaking to Audrey.

"I would never have bet money on Ike dancing in a million years." From Hiroshi talking to Miku.

"Go, Isaac! Go, Isaac! Who the hell knew the white boy could dance?" from Carlton talking to Simon.

"Come on, darlin'. I don't have to sit here and listen to this."

Sidney laughed as he took her hand and led her away.

"What do you say we make two hopeful people very happy right now?"

She looked into his eyes. "What do you mean?"

Isaac shrugged a shoulder.

"I was thinking of asking my mama to dance."

He breathed out a nervous breath, and Sidney's heart melted.

"Oh, Ike. I think she would love that!"

"Yeah?"

"Yes."

"Well, I think Carlton might like it too."

Sidney glanced across the room to where the man sat at a table talking to Simon and Ike's boss, Gavin.

"What do you say?"

"Okay."

He kissed her lips, and then he left her and walked over to where his mother and father were sitting talking to Emily and Agent Fox. Audrey smiled when Ike interrupted them. She couldn't hear what they said, but the light on her new mother-in-law's face was priceless and endearing.

Isaac offered her his arm, not his hand, and Audrey took it as she stood.

He led her over to their private dance floor, and Sidney walked over to Carlton.

"Excuse me gentlemen, I'm sorry to interrupt. But I was wondering if you'd dance with me?"

Carlton looked up at her, and then did a double take when she offered him her hand.

"Me?"

She smiled and nodded.

"Yes! I'd be honored."

He took her hand and she led him to the private dance floor to join Ike and Audrey just as the music changed to "Lullaby for Wyatt," by Sheryl Crow.

"Thank you for this, Sidney. I truly appreciate it."

"You make it sound like I'm doing you a favor."

"Aren't you?"

"No. I wanted to dance with my dad at my wedding."

Carlton stopped dancing for a second and looked at her.

"I do believe that's the first time you've called me that since I've been here."

They resumed dancing.

"I'm sorry."

"No, don't be. I get it. I haven't earned the right to be called that by you or Simon. And that's okay. I'm just happy you've both given me a chance to know you. That's all I was after."

"I heard Simon is going to have a look at your scans? Show them to a colleague of his. A specialist."

"Yeah, he asked to."

"Is that a problem for you?"

"Why would it be a problem? Extra eyes. Fresh eyes. Hell, maybe they'll spot something that'll help, and I won't be staring at a death sentence."

"It would be nice to have you around for a while so we could talk some more. Get to know each other better."

"I would love that. Truly."

"Well, maybe it'll happen."

He smiled at her.

"Congratulations, babygirl. It was a beautiful wedding. I even took off my shoes and buried my toes in the sand."

Sidney laughed, and he kissed her cheek.

They danced with their parents for two full songs before taking a break from the dance floor. As they sat sipping non-alcoholic champagne and feeding each other, Sterling wandered over to their table, beaming at them.

"It was an absolutely beautiful ceremony. You two have made an old man deliriously happy."

"Thank you, Grandad. I'm so happy you were here to celebrate with us."

"Me too, Sterling." Sidney smiled at him. "Thank you for being here."

"Well, you can thank me by facilitating introductions to the fetching woman sitting at the next table."

Sidney and Isaac turned to see who Sterling was talking about. Then they looked at each other with surprised expressions.

"Ah, Grandad, you..."

"She is friend of yours, yes?"

"Well, yes, she is, but..."

"There's something about her I find intriguing. Who is she?"

"She's... well, she's... um..."

Clearly, Isaac was having a hard time with this. So Sidney leaned over and motioned to the woman, getting her attention.

"Geneviève! Come sit with us. There's someone I want you to meet."

Geneviève smiled and wafted over, her purple flowery dress flowing to her ankles. The bangles at her wrists jingled like happy bells. Her long red hair was twisted into a fancy braid and adorned with daisies, and she wore a large amethyst on a chain around her neck.

"Sidney, you look just beautiful!"

"Thank you." Sidney hugged the woman.

"And Isaac. So dashing. It was a beautiful ceremony."

"Thanks, Geneviève." Isaac sounded less than gracious.

"Thank you for inviting me!"

"Geneviève, we'd like you to meet Isaac's grandfather, Sterling Taylor. Sterling, this is Geneviève Leroux."

Sterling and Geneviève looked at one another, and she reached out her hand.

Sterling hesitated for a split second before he reached out with his cotton-gloved hand.

"So you are the hypersensitive psychic that Isaac inherited his gift from?" Geneviève smiled at him.

"And you must be the delightful psychic mentor my grandson's been telling me about. It's a pleasure to meet you, my dear."

They smiled at each other, and Sidney watched Isaac sag a little bit, as if deflated.

As the afternoon slipped into early evening, she and Isaac cut the beautiful lemon flavored wedding cake with blueberry filling. It had been adorned with edible sea shells and pearls, and it was perfect.

After cake and more mingling, Isaac wrapped his arms around Sidney from behind as she was talking to her cousin, Erika.

"I hate to break up this party, but we have a plane to catch in about two hours. We need to get changed and head to the airport."

"Are you finally going to tell me where we're going?"

"Not just yet. Once we're in the car."

"Promise?"

"Would I ever lie to you, my darlin' wife?"

Sidney turned around in his embrace and hooked her arms around his neck.

"No, my amazing, sexy husband. You would not."

She let him lead her off to the changing rooms, where they each changed into more suitable travel attire — she into a little white dress that hit her at mid-thigh and sported peasant sleeves. And he into a light brown suit and a white dress shirt with no tie.

Their bags were already tucked into the trunk of the limo, so when they emerged in their post wedding attire, they said their goodbyes to their family and friends.

Sidney thanked her aunt, uncle, and cousins for coming all the way from California.

They thanked Adam and Bree for everything.

Birdseed was tossed as they left the reception and rushed to the waiting limo.

Sidney and Isaac both fell back against the seat with a collective sigh.

"We did it."

"Yes, we did."

"We're actually married, Ike."

"Yes, we are."

"And the venue didn't get wiped out by a freak tsunami. The beach didn't get covered in water. It didn't rain. The roses in the rose garden didn't die. There were no other disasters."

"Nope." Isaac took her hand, lacing their fingers together. "Nothing but blue skies and starry nights."

She looked over at him and smiled.

He leaned in and kissed her lips.

"Now will you tell me where we're going?"

"Okay." He reached into the pocket of his suit jacket and pulled out their plane tickets and handed them to her.

Sidney examined the tickets with care.

A lightning bolt set off a small fire in her belly.

"Oh, my God."

Her gaze shot up to his.

"Is this for real?"

"It is."

"Hawaii?"

"You don't like Hawaii?"

"I'm sure I'll love Hawaii! I've never been. It just never occurred to me that we'd be going anywhere so grand. I mean I know it's technically still America, but it feels like another country to me!"

She knew she was babbling now, and Isaac just laughed at her.

"Well, I've never been before either. But according to Adam, the island of Lanai is like some tropical paradise or something. Private beaches and a luxury resort. And I know how much you love the Pacific Ocean, so I thought you might want to see it from the other side."

Sidney squealed. She couldn't help it. Then she practically threw herself forward and into Ike's lap. She threaded her fingers through his hair and kissed his lips.

"I'm so excited!"

"Good. I'm glad you're excited. I love you, darlin'."

"I love you back, baby. So much it hurts."

EPILOGUE

*S*idney laid back on the lounge chair and stretched, her lithe body glistening in the Hawaiian sun, and Isaac watched her as though he were watching his favorite show on TV.

Her every move captivated him and turned him on.

They'd spent much of the first week of their honeymoon just making love and taking cat naps all day long. They canoodled everywhere — in their honeymoon suite, in their private cabana on the beach, and in the double lounge chair that sat on the terrace just outside their suite. They'd even stumbled on a secluded cove during one of their long walks on the beach where they'd made good use of the hidden inlet.

Isaac couldn't help himself. He was like a rabbit, or a horny teenager, or a man who'd gone most of his life deprived of all physical human touch.

He was only grateful that Sidney didn't seem to mind too much. Whenever he reached for her, she gave herself willingly. Taking him deeper, higher, further, with every sensual encounter.

He was making an effort this week though. They had plans to do some sight seeing or island activity each day. Today it had been snorkeling, and they'd loved the beautiful coral reefs they'd seen.

Tomorrow, they were taking a day trip to Kauai by helicopter to do a little shopping.

They were lying on the beach now looking out at the ocean, and Isaac turned on his side to face her. He reached out a hand and ran his finger down her toned belly.

"I need to tell you something, darlin'."

Sidney opened her eyes and looked up at him. Her golden champagne-colored eyes sparkled in the sun.

"Yes, my love?"

"A confession of sorts."

"A confession?"

"Um hmm."

"Okay?"

Isaac drew tiny circles on her stomach with his finger, and she giggled and swatted at his hand. The sound made him smile.

"Well, do you remember the night we met in person for the first time?"

"At the Italian restaurant where my car was blown up. Of course."

"Yeah. Well... do you remember when we shook hands and I kind of reacted funny?"

"Because you saw something with your superpowers when you touched my hand?"

Isaac's gaze met hers.

"Yeah."

"I remember. I didn't know what it meant at the time, but I knew something significant had happened."

"You're right. Something significant had happened. Something very significant."

She reached up and caressed his cheek, and Isaac leaned his face into her hand.

"So, what was it? What did you see?"

Isaac took a deep breath and looked into her eyes.

"I saw you. Barefoot on the beach."

"Oh, yeah. You told me that once."

Isaac nodded. "But I didn't tell you the whole story. See, that was only part of what I saw in that flash."

"Well, what else did you see?"

"You were barefoot, walking towards me. Your white dress and your hair blowing in the soft breeze. You took my hand and smiled at me."

"That sounds nice."

"Yeah. But then later at my place, when we were making love, I saw it again. That same vision of you on the beach. Only that time I saw the whole picture. The white dress. I saw the flowers and the golden bubbles of the champagne."

"Champagne?"

"I saw our wedding, Sidney. The very first time we met in person and I touched your hand, the vision I saw was of you and me at our wedding."

"Isaac."

They stared into each other's eyes for a long moment.

"That's why you never wanted to tell me what you saw that day. Because…"

"Because I didn't want to influence you in any way." He ran a finger under her chin and interrupted her. Then he took her hand. "If this was going to happen, I wanted to be sure that it happened because it was something *you* wanted. Not something we were doing just to make my vision true. I wanted to know that you were marrying me because you love me, Sidney."

"Oh, baby, I do. I love you so much, Isaac."

He kissed her hand, and then her lips.

"I can't believe you've been having visions of our wedding all this time."

"I couldn't believe it either. In fact, I didn't believe it. Not really. Not until I reconnected with my grandad and he said things."

"What things?"

Isaac shrugged his shoulders.

"Things like telling me to cherish you always, and how happy he was that I'd found my shield. How much better you were going to make my life. That's when I knew... like really *knew* that my flashes of us on that beach were real. That I was really seeing the future, and that you were meant to be my wife."

Sidney smiled at him, and then she wrapped her body around him and snuggled in close. Isaac tightened his embrace, pulling her even closer.

"I love the fact that I was meant only for you, Isaac."

He grinned at her and gently placed his forehead on hers.

"I love that too, darlin'. And I love you so very much."

"I love you back, baby."

"I can't wait to see what the future holds for us, Mrs. Taylor."

"Well, you do have psychic superpowers, Mr. Taylor. Concentrate, and maybe it'll come to you."

Isaac smiled, and then he kissed her.

***

NOTE FROM LASHELL

It's been a whirlwind from that wrong number phone call of book 1 to this beach wedding and honeymoon, *but they made it!* When I started writing the Isaac Taylor Mystery Series, I had no idea if readers were going to like it or not. I mean, let's be honest... Isaac Taylor is a pretty unusual romantic hero.

Strange abilities that he's afraid of, touch issues, recovering alcoholic, awkward with the ladies. I had no clue if readers would see all the good things in Isaac that I see.

I also wasn't sure if readers would like Sidney either. She doesn't exactly start out as a badass, and I know how much readers hate a weak heroine. But these two lost souls came to me raw and broken, and told me their story. I had to write it they way they instructed.

And I'll continue to do exactly that, for however long Ike & Sid keep talking to me. That's right. There is still plenty more story to tell with these two. Marriage is just the beginning!

So, thank you for reading *Curses & Vows*. If you're enjoying reading the continuing romance between Isaac and Sidney, CLICK HERE to download book 7, *Scandals & Love Songs* now!

JOIN LASHELL'S FACEBOOK READER GROUP

Want to get the scoop (like blurbs, release dates, cover reveals, etc.) on all of Lashell's newest books before anyone else? Want dibs on being the first to read and review her latest releases? Want to hang out and ask her questions about her books, or join a community of other readers to discuss favorite characters and plot points? Then joining her Facebook Reader Group is the way to do it! Click the link below to join.

https://www.facebook.com/groups/853329598037117/

ACKNOWLEDGMENTS

Cover Design by Sonia Freitas of
www.chloebellearts.com

ABOUT THE AUTHOR

Lashell Collins is an American author of romantic suspense, paranormal romance, and rockstar romance. She walks to the beat of her own drum, but that's okay 'cause she's got a pretty good sense of rhythm. Basically, she's a geeky, quirky, laid-back, rocker-loving kinda girl who's married to a retired cop, motorcycle-riding, bad-boy alpha all her own, and she likes to write about sexy werewolves, rockstars or police officers, or some inventive combination of the three. Between her book characters and the ones she knows in real life, her plate stays pretty full. But she loves to hear from readers, so connect with her in the following ways:

Newsletter Sign-up:
http://www.lashellcollins.com/newsletter
Website:
http://lashellcollins.com

ALSO BY LASHELL COLLINS

Jagged Ivory Series **(Rockstar Romance)**

Jagged Hearts

Jagged Dreams

Jagged Addiction

Jagged Secrets

Jagged Surrender

Kelly Family Series **(Romantic Suspense)**

Ethan: A Kelly Family Novella

Storm: A Kelly Family Novella

Frankie: A Kelly Family Novella

Marina: A Kelly Family Novella

Where There's Smoke: A Kelly Family Novel

The Smoking Gun: A Kelly Family Novel

Lunar Falls Trilogy **(Paranormal Romance)**

Secrets of Lunar Falls

Lies of Lunar Falls

Redemption of Lunar Falls

Exiled: A Lunar Falls Novella

Rock Shifter Fairytales **(Paranormal/Rockstar Romance)**

Soul Stealer

Lion Tamer

She Wolf

The Raven

Rogue Moon Series **(Paranormal Romance)**

Rogue Moon

Fated Moon

True Romance Series **(Rockstar Romance)**

True Romance

All Fired Up

Isaac Taylor Mysteries **(Romantic Suspense)**

Voices & Visions

Lovers & Monsters

Freaks & Family Legacies

Lullabies & Dead Bodies

Murders & Romance